NO GOOD STUFF IN THE BOOK OF JOB

NO GOOD STUFF IN THE BOOK OF JOB

KEN TEUTSCH

Square2 Books

1

Frankly, the Call to Keep Tennessee Safe for Christianity couldn't have come at a worse time.

It wasn't that David Burkitt didn't *want* to keep Tennessee safe for Christianity, at least in theory; it was just that at the moment he had a lot of other things on his mind, foremost among them the recent collapse of his entire world. David's was a mind that was unused to being so crowded. Not to imply that he was a dunce or anything; no, he was a reasonably intelligent fellow. He had a college degree. He juggled numbers and did financial calculations for a living. It was just that he had until recently—very recently— only a relatively few things to really be concerned about, all orderly and properly arranged, the most complex of which (the ongoing changes in the tax code) mainly kept track of, if the truth be known, via software updates. Yet at the moment the Call came, the inside of David's head was working like a popcorn popper.

He considered ignoring the Call. Almost anyone would have, given the long-term and largely speculative nature of the menace to Christianity as opposed to the acute and imperative nature of his current, ongoing world collapse. But then, both history and scripture, which many people feel are largely one and the same, tell us that it is in the nature of such a Call to arrive when the one called is unready, or in the nature of people in general to never be quite ready for such a Call whenever it comes. In this case, of course, David was not really prepared for a call of any kind, capitalized or otherwise.

This call probably shouldn't actually be capitalized. It was not a spiritual Call, or a Call directly from God. It was not a voice from a burning bush or even just a voice in David's head, either of which, statistically speaking, would be more likely schizophrenic than supernatural in any case. This call was a regular, uncapitalized call on a telephone—a landline, at that. But the capitalized name on the caller I.D. capitalized the Call in David's mind and made him afraid to answer it but more afraid not to, much as actual Calls directly from God are said to have affected many recipients over the years. Afraid-not-to won out, and he did answer it, though his "Hello" came out more as a croak than as a human voice speaking English. The voice that replied, in contrast, was such a beautifully modulated baritone that one might have been forgiven for thinking it was that of God himself after all, God having ineffably chosen to make his Calls using a landline.

"David!" said the lovely voice. "Raymond." The upward lilt of the first word together with the rolling downward swoop of the second were as close to an aria as one could get using only four notes. The melody continued, "We're about to have a little last-minute meeting about tonight and tomorrow. Consensus was that we should bring you in on it. Can you come on down to the station?"

David cleared his throat. He realized how badly the "hello" had come out, and he wanted his explanation for why he couldn't possibly make it to any meeting to come out more clearly. Except that he didn't have an explanation for why he couldn't make it. That is, he had a very good *reason*, but he was not prepared to give it. He was not yet, in fact, prepared even to believe it himself. Also, as he was a very poor and inexperienced liar, fabricating an explanation, plausible or otherwise, on the spur of the moment was utterly beyond him.

Such an explanation would have been wasted had he come up with it, since Reverend Raymond Dumond, who was the person behind the beautiful voice, did not pause for a reply, the possibility of a refusal having never entered his mind. He simply went on. "We'll see you over here in a half-hour or so, then. God bless."

When Raymond Dumond said, "God bless," there was a tremendous amount of context jammed into the words. First, there was the implication that God had confided in Raymond Dumond personally, and that Raymond Dumond was simply passing along the news. In fact, his voice seemed to indicate, God had in some sense already blessed you simply by allowing you into the presence of Raymond Dumond. On the other hand, there was also a hint of reticence, a sense of the conditional, as though after the assurance of God's blessing there hung in the air the unspoken words, "...unless of course you disappoint...Raymond Dumond."

Hanging in the air after this particular "God bless" were the plain old spoken words, "As I was saying..." These words Raymond Dumond spoke to whomever was in the room with him and were followed by a terminal, yet somehow celestial, *click*.

David was wearing a stricken look when he lifted the phone, and he added another thick coat of stricken on top of that as he put it down. Like many before him who had received more legitimately capitalized Calls, he considered resisting this one. But before the phone rang and David pounced on it, recoiled from it, then reluctantly answered it, he had already been standing there in his kitchen for quite a while, frozen, a crumpled piece of paper in his hand, wearing his business casual khakis, blue shirt, pale-yellow-with-blue-dots tie and stricken look, gazing about at the black, white and red of the room and the things in it, including the impatiently mewling cat, utterly at a loss as to what to do next. This summons from Reverend Dumond was badly timed and unwanted, but it was at least a stimulus to move. The alternative seemed to be to stand there like a stump for the rest of his life. So David went.

Things would almost certainly have gone much better for him had he not.

2

"Hey, Dave!"

David was startled by several things. He was standing staring placidly at a fuzzy, red rectangle, not thinking much of anything at all, when Jeremy appeared, startlingly, at his side. He was startled by Jeremy's appearance, and startled to find himself standing in the TV station hallway, since he didn't recall how he got down there. But most of all, he was startled by Jeremy's blurted question.

"You seen Glenda?"

Jeremy was one of only two full-time employees, not counting the owner/managers, at Channel 38, which was the television station in the hallway of which David found himself materialized. Channel 38 was a low-power religious television station, most of the programming of which was produced at a much larger sister station in Lexington, Kentucky. Some, however, was produced by local volunteers. Jeremy's title was Chief Engineer, which meant he had the responsibility of calling in a real engineer should any of the equipment malfunction, and of keeping an eye on the various volunteers who ran the control room, generally overseeing everything technical about the local productions, and handling the editing and graphics. The only other full-time employee outside of management was Laura, the receptionist. Or rather, Administrative Assistant. She became hostile–more hostile than usual–if called a receptionist.

Jeremy was a few years younger than David's thirty-two and seemed even younger than that because of his long hair, his beard, and his tendency to dress in jeans and t-shirts with clever sayings rather than in what David might have judged to be professional attire. Jeremy's current t-shirt was gray. It said, "YOU *[large picture of a mustache]* ME ABOUT JESUS." David had no idea what that was supposed to mean.

Jeremy's *You seen Glenda?* was an odd thing to be asked of David at any time; today it was not merely odd, but sure-enough startling. It was so startling in fact, especially in combination with everything else, that David actually started—that is, jumped a half-step to one side and brought his hands up defensively, as though Jeremy had thrust a snake at him rather than a query. For his part, Jeremy assumed that the start was merely the result of his sudden appearance, so he raised his own hands in an apologetic gesture and said, "Sorry, man! Didn't mean to startle ya."

He repeated then his odd question. "You seen Glenda?"

David didn't feel up to making eye contact, so he looked back down the hall at the red rectangle which had earlier been so fuzzy and indistinct. It became once more fuzzy and indistinct as he pondered Jeremy's odd question. "Hey, Dave! You seen Glenda?" was odd because Glenda was David Burkitt's wife. The two of them had the number one show on Channel 38: *The Light in Your Life*. And who asks a husband as he walks in the door, "Hey, Dave! Have you seen your wife?" Why *wouldn't* he have seen his wife? She was his wife!

The problem was, he had not seen his wife.

Also, nobody called him "Dave."

The fuzzy rectangle David was mindlessly contemplating was a poster push-pinned to the wall at the end of the entrance hallway next to the Ficus plant. Jeremy was, in fact, the person who had put the poster there. Jeremy was a great admirer of catchy slogans and clever catchphrases, on t-shirts and elsewhere. The poster was three feet high and bright red. It featured a white silhouette of a crown made of thorns, beneath which, in white block letters, were the words:

KEEP
CALM
and
TRUST
JESUS

The letters resolved themselves now as David waited for Jeremy to go away and as Jeremy continued to not do so, and he read them rather than just seeing them. *Keep Calm and Trust Jesus.* David thought about it. Good advice. And he did trust Jesus. His crisis had not yet approached a level that could put a dent in that.

He was, however, finding it harder and harder to keep calm.

"Thing is..." Jeremy went on, "I thought she was gonna meet me last night. To take a look at the promo. The promo we were working on, you know?" He jerked a thumb over his shoulder toward the nearby edit bay. "But she didn't, and then I texted her. Like, you know...several times. And..." He made vague circles in the air with both hands. He sounded worried.

"Oh? Really?" Glenda had been out late the previous evening, and David had been under the impression that she *had* been working on the promo. He tried again for a second to make eye contact with Jeremy, found that utterly unbearable, and so returned his gaze to the poster, as though he had not seen it hundreds of times before. "I guess she must have got busy."

Jeremy persisted in not going away. He shifted from one foot to the other and rubbed his hands together to warm them, though it was actually somewhat too warm there in the hallway already, or at least seemed so to David. Because the control room was kept especially cool for the machinery, and because Jeremy apparently could not bear to obscure the clever sayings on his t-shirts with sweater or jacket, he was often vigorously rubbing his hands and arms or stamping his feet like a Minneapolis beat cop on a January night. "She's OK, though?" he said, blowing on his fingers. "Glenda always... I mean, she never just..."

Glenda always *what*? Kept her promises? Glenda never just *what*? Disappeared? David found himself feeling uncharitably negative thoughts about Jeremy. But that wasn't really fair, was it? "Uh huh," he said. "Fine. I've got to go, Jeremy. I've got a meeting with Reverend Dumond."

"Yeah?" Jeremy took a step back and looked down the hall toward the reception desk. He rarely ventured into the inner sanctum where the offices were. "Oh. About the Thing?" he said, meaning the Rally to Keep Tennessee Safe for Christianity. "Sure. Right. Just tell Glenda that I was asking about her, OK?" He started backing away toward the control room door. "About the promo, I mean. We can re-schedule." He made a waggling "call-me" sign with one hand next to the side of his head.

"You bet. Will do." David moved away down the hallway, frowning. He took a deep breath and stopped for a few more seconds before the large, red poster, then turned to the reception desk. Laura was there as usual, and did not look up or greet him, as also usual. "Hi, Laura," he said. "Got a meeting with Reverend Dumond. I mean, there's a meeting. I guess."

Laura nodded at her computer screen as though his voice had come from there. Laura's hair was a sort of brick-red today, but David was fairly sure it had been a different shade the last time he saw her. She was wearing a yellow dress and a necklace that looked as though it was made from the floor sweepings of a high school metal shop. The dress seemed to be just a tad on the small side given Laura's build, and every time she shifted in her chair one hand went automatically to yank and pull at the hem. Glenda had said on one occasion that Laura dressed "too young for herself." David did not feel qualified to judge, nor to gauge Laura's age, for that matter, other than having the vague idea that she was older than himself.

She glanced up at last, and her eyes darted about at the empty space surrounding David before meeting his own. "Just you?" She looked at him oddly, and there was also something odd in her tone. It seemed even colder than usual.

"Hm?" David said. "Oh. Yes. I just... We, uh..."

"He's in there already," Laura interrupted. "Everybody's in there already." She went back to ignoring him and stabbing at her keyboard somewhat viciously with one orange fingernail.

"Just me," David mumbled, and he found himself now having uncharitably negative thoughts about Laura.

David Burkitt was of the feeling that we are all God's creatures and none of us perfect. Therefore, he was quite strict with himself about having uncharitable thoughts. Hearing himself thinking those uncharitable thoughts about Laura sent his mind into an automatic litany of self-correction. *Judge not that ye be not judged,* he thought. That was one of his favorites. Matthew 7, verse 1. He liked a lot of Matthew, come to think of it. Chapter Seven in particular. Lots of Good Stuff in Matthew. Lots of red print in his Bible with Jesus' words in red print, red print therefore being always a sign of Good Stuff. David was a King James man. He didn't care for modern updated translations. He liked it when Jesus said, "Verily, I say unto you." He didn't like it when Jesus said, "Yo, listen up!" Now he ran his eyes over the red print in his mind, the room around him becoming as fuzzy as the poster had been earlier.

Whosoever is angry at his brother without a cause shall be in danger of the judgment... That was Good Stuff.

Matthew's red print scrolled by faster.

Love your enemies. Bless them that curse you...

Ye shall know them by their fruits...

What therefore God hath joined together, let no man put asunder...

David sobbed. It came out of nowhere, taking him completely by surprise, and he coughed loudly in an attempt to camouflage it. "Be right back!" he choked as he lunged toward the door to the restroom just beyond Laura's desk. He stumbled into the stall, sat on the toilet and began to weep, his head slowly sinking into his hands.

3

That morning David got up early because he had an appointment. He had a small office in a room built onto their garage where people came in and sat across the desk while he tap, tap, tapped on a keyboard, filling out tax forms they could often just as easily have filled out themselves. But he had a few bigger clients with real accounting needs, and when they needed consultation, he generally went to them. This was the case today with a man down in a nearby town who owned three laundromats.

He quickly fed the cat to stop it yowling and moved quietly about the house getting ready. Glenda was still asleep. He wasn't sure when she had come to bed the night before; she had been out all evening at one of her club meetings and at the TV station, came in late and then was up even later doing stuff on her computer. She had her own computer in a little alcove off the dining room where she wheeled and dealed online in Coca-Cola memorabilia, and she had explained that she had to do much of her wheeling and dealing in the wee hours because many of the other collectors were in far away, exotic time zones. So most mornings, even mornings when he did not rise especially early, he was careful not to disturb her. Before leaving, he looked one more time into the bedroom. Only a tangle of brown hair was visible on the rumpled pillow. Glenda's fuzzy, blue bathrobe lay draped across the foot of the bed. He smiled and quietly closed the door.

When he walked back into the house a few hours later, he called out, but she didn't answer. He looked into the bedroom and saw that the bed, unmade, was empty. The fuzzy, blue bathrobe was still draped across the foot. He moved through the house, calling her in a progressively louder voice. He went to the garage and saw that Glenda's car was there. He went back to the bedroom where he had started. This time he noticed that the jewelry box that sat upon the dresser, that had *always* sat upon the dresser, the box Glenda had had since childhood with the ballerina which had once twirled when the lid was opened but which no longer did so, was gone. His eye caught then the open closet door and a pile of hangers on the floor. He turned on the closet light. Most of Glenda's clothes were gone.

His throat closed and he caught his breath. His first thought was: burglary. It did not occur to him to find it odd that nothing was stolen except Glenda's belongings. He ran through the house now, calling her name loudly, the question mark after it emphasized very, *very* loudly, his heartbeat accelerating with each echo uninterrupted by any reply. He charged out the back door and surveyed the empty back yard, empty porch, empty lawn chairs, barely able to stop himself from shouting her name into the morning sky.

He finally stopped the aimless circling and stood in the kitchen. Should he call 911? The cat, Bitsy, an overweight black-and-white creature with one droopy eye, sat in the middle of the dining table next to a tiny, impressively detailed model of a vintage Coca-Cola vending machine. Bitsy had watched his running about with her usual detached disinterest, but now gave a burbling, phlegmy, "Murro," assuming, as cats will, that David must have come into the room to give her something to eat, and so should get on with it. David reached for the telephone, but as he glanced toward the table, he finally noticed the sheet of paper beneath the tiny Coke machine. He had missed it hitherto because it was nearly completely obscured by Bitsy's broad, fuzzy haunches. With some effort, and after provoking a certain amount of hissing, he managed to shift the cat enough to snatch the paper up. He stood in the middle of the room and read it, his breaths coming faster and shallower until his head began to swim.

Their kitchen had been decorated by Glenda so as to resemble an archetypal yet still somehow fantastical 1950s diner, the better to create an appropriate setting for the display of her collection of vintage Coca-Cola memorabilia. The floor was a black and white checkerboard, somewhat dizzying even when one was not hyperventilating. The table was faux-vintage chrome and red Formica, the chairs red vinyl. Coca-Cola themed signs covered the walls. Coca-Cola themed doodads crowded the doo-dad shelves near the ceiling. Coca-Cola themed magnets covered the refrigerator like barnacles on a man-o-war. "It's the Real Thing!" shouted a metal sign. "Perfect Harmony," said a hippie-looking girl. "Things go better," laughed a ruddy, squinty-eyed Santa Claus. David, looking up after reading the paper, found that Coca-Cola, it suddenly seemed, had to be about the most ironic soft drink in the world.

He still held this piece of paper retrieved from under the cat and the Coke machine as he stood a few minutes later, stricken, frozen near the telephone, when it rang with The Call (or rather, the call). He was standing near the telephone when it rang because he had just been using it to call Glenda's cell phone. He had called repeatedly and unsuccessfully from his own cell phone and thought, illogically, that maybe the landline would work better. It hadn't. David had heard people in the past, angry people, wish other people would go "straight to Hell!" There in his kitchen, handset squeezed in sweaty palm, he considered that curse to be nothing compared to, "straight to voicemail."

That same piece of paper, more crumpled than previously, he now pulled from his pocket there in the Channel 38 bathroom stall. There was no point in doing this. It wasn't as though the message was going to have changed, or that some sort of invisible ink would have mysteriously appeared since the last time he looked, supplying a punchline to what would be a decidedly unfunny joke.

Dear David, I am sorry to hurt you this way...

The door to the restroom opened with a bang, and a shadow swept across the floor outside the stall. Large, muddy boots came into view in the gap under the door. David jumped and re-crumpled the already crumpled paper. He jumped again, higher this time, when a fist thudded, BAM BAM BAM on the stall door.

"You all right in there?" said a low, gravelly voice.

"I, uh, ulp, yes!" David stammered in shock.

"Laura said you run in here like you was sick," the voice rumbled. "Got the trots or something?"

"No!" David stood and jammed the piece of paper back into his pocket. He recognized the voice now. It was Rolly Blaney. What was he doing here?

"Well, meeting's started." David had completely forgotten that he was here for the meeting. The meeting about the effort to Keep Tennessee Safe for Christianity. So of course Blaney would be here, too. David ran a shaky hand over his eyes and prepared to try to speak, then started once again even more violently than he had when startled by Jeremy. What startled him was the large, brown, somewhat bloodshot eye peering at him through the crack at the edge of the stall door.

"Say," Blaney growled, "You seen Glenda?"

4

How the whole "Keep Tennessee Safe for Christianity" project the organization of which dragged the crisis-wracked David Burkitt and his letter with the distinctly ominous opening line out of his house and down to the TV station bathroom came about was: Their town was home to a small state college, and between international faculty (largely teaching science and engineering) and international students (largely studying science and engineering), there had come to be enough people around there who practiced the Muslim religion—something until recently completely unknown in the area—that they decided to pitch in and lease and renovate an old, disused dental clinic on Lakeview Road and turn it into a Muslim Community Center. Which they did.

Various members of this religious community proceeded to congregate there on Fridays and to take part in various holiday observances, community events and so forth there, and had done so for quite some time, during which span nobody much noticed or, if they did notice, particularly cared or, if they did care, considered doing anything about it. Then, one recent afternoon, Rolly Blaney, the fellow destined to so startle David Burkitt there in the Channel 38 restroom, happened to drive past the place. He had driven past the place before, but this time he happened to notice the sign.

When he noticed the sign he could not at first believe his eyes, so he locked up his brakes—which he could do because he drove a pale blue Ford pickup truck designed and built before the days of anti-lock brakes—and ground his standard transmission (with the shifter on the steering column) into reverse to careen in a serpentine manner back to where he could get another look. Luckily, there was no other traffic on the road at that time, since Blaney certainly didn't check his mirrors first. A second look confirmed what his glance had first perceived: A hand-painted white sign with a black star and crescent moon and the words, "Boyd County Islamic Center" in regular American letters next to Allah only knew what in squiggly Arabic letters.

"You have got," said Rolly Blaney, "to be shitting me."

But of course, as explained earlier, they weren't.

Rolly Blaney, whose given name was actually Rolf after his paternal grandfather, who (grandfather Rolf, that is) had worn an eyepatch after losing sight in one eye from a beating he received in 1917 for being a kraut, and whose middle name (Rolly's, that is) was Joseph after his mother's grandfather, whose name was originally Giuseppe, and who died in a mine collapse in West Virginia because they sent the wops into the most dangerous tunnels, and whose last name, Blaney, had actually been adopted by grandpa Rolf from his wife, whose people were micks, because being even a mick in America in 1917 was safer than being a kraut, did not like foreigners.

Most especially, he did not like dark-skinned foreigners. More specifically, he *really* did not like Muslim foreigners, and he considered all Muslims to be foreigners, even the ones who were born here. (So, incidentally, he would not have cared, had he known about him, for his great-great grandfather on his mother's side, Youssef, who was a sailor from Tunisia and who met Rolly's maternal great-great grandmother briefly, but luckily for Rolly not *that* briefly, while on leave from a cargo ship in Palermo.)

Hence his immediate, traffic-laws-be-damned outrage upon learning that some Muslims had a Community Center in Boyd County.

When he ground his truck's transmission back into first and peeled out forward again, Rolly Blaney was a Tunisian-Italian-

German-Irish all-American Christian on a Mission. Which mission ultimately, or at least eventually, led to:

5

David following Blaney, who was dressed as though he just came from either duck hunting or infiltrating a Central American country (except for his cap, which was bright red and would have been a liability while ambushing either mallards or Sandinistas), into Raymond Dumond's office. The office was technically that of Deion Mullins, the Station Manager at Channel 38, but everything at the station was Raymond Dumond's when Raymond Dumond was on the premises, so at the moment the office was Raymond Dumond's office, and the desk he rose from was his desk. It was his velvet voice which said, "Hello, David. Sorry about the short notice."

Dumond's age was unguessable. He was either a young man who looked older than his years or an older man who looked younger than his years. Either way the effect was one of sage wisdom mixed with glowing vitality. His hair was dark, of a moderate length and simply gorgeous. His smile was stunning. At least it stunned David, who replied, "You're welcome."

There was at that time a trend among pastors towards more casual attire, but Raymond Dumond, founder and pastor of The Great Rock Church, managed to dress informally while somehow still looking impeccable. The Reverend wore a checked shirt and blue jeans. The jeans looked brand new and indefinably better than normal jeans. The shirt was somehow vaguely more shirty than a regular shirt. His supple, almost luminous, brown shoes had most certainly not been purchased at Payless or Shoe Carnival.

David heard that his own voice was dry and crackly once again. He was, if possible, even more addled now than at any point that morning. With Rolly Blaney looming outside the stall he hadn't been able to continue to hide in the restroom, which he would have liked to do, possibly forever, and his brain was now scrambled by the strain of his attempt and failure to conjure up an answer to that second unlooked-for, "You seen Glenda?" All he had said was, "Aha!" Blaney had led him out of the room with an openly suspicious look on his darkly stubbled face.

Deion, the station manager, and his wife, Mary, who functioned as his de facto assistant manager, sat on the loveseat against the wall. They sat forward on the seat cushions, backs straight, hands clasped in their laps like attentive schoolchildren. Mary smiled at David, a tight, lips-only smile. Deion was stocky, about forty, with a thin mustache and a perennially serious demeanor, which David attributed to the pressures of his job, though he had no idea what those might be. Mary was a friendly, cheerful woman, a few years older than her husband, and considerably wider. Deion and Mary were African American, and the only non-White people, employee or volunteer, associated with Channel 38. Reverend Dumond often pointed to them (sometimes literally) to indicate his Church's media organization's inclusivity and lack of bias.

To David's surprise, sitting next to Mary, wedged into the scant remaining space on the loveseat, was Brother Horace Birdsong, the minister of the town's First Baptist Church. Brother Birdsong smiled cordially at David, and David began to blush as he always did when he encountered Brother Birdsong nowadays.

"He was in the can," said Blaney, and he plopped into the only other chair in the room and crossed his right leg onto his left knee. A chunk of dried mud dislodged from the sole of his boot and fell with a slight *thump* onto the carpet.

"Have a seat," Dumond told David, taking his place once more on the corner of the desk.

"Glenda not with you?" asked Deion.

Again? David felt short of breath. "No, um, she's... She was..." He stepped farther into the room to take a seat, but there was no seat to take. "Not right now." He looked helplessly about for a moment, then moved over to perch on the arm of the loveseat next to Brother Birdsong.

"I was just telling Reverend Birdsong," said Dumond, "how glad we are that he's joined us." He smiled his beatific smile at the Baptist minister.

Brother Birdsong cleared his throat and tried and failed to squirm into a more upright position from the crack in the loveseat cushions he found himself sinking into. "For the meeting," he said. "I've joined you...for the meeting."

"Exactly," said Dumond, and his smile tightened almost imperceptibly. "Now that we're pretty much all here...let's start with—"

"Actually," Brother Birdsong interrupted, "if I could just..." He wriggled again, and Deion and Mary tried unsuccessfully to scootch down to give him more room. He grabbed at David's arm. "May I?" he said, and pulled, nearly dragging David off the arm of the loveseat, but using the leverage finally extricated himself from the cushion crack in order to sit up. "If I could just say something?" he said.

"Oh, here we go," muttered Blaney.

"I came over here to suggest to you," Brother Birdsong began, but he was brought up short by Rolly Blaney's hostile gaze. He switched his attention to Brother Dumond. "...To ask you to reconsider this...whatever it is you have planned. I really believe it's unnecessary and will probably actually be, uh, counterproductive."

Rolly Blaney made a noise between a grunt and a snort.

"Well, Horace," said Dumond after a pause, "I'm a little disappointed. I had hoped you had come to say that First Baptist stood with us in this work."

"Well, I want to. I want to stand with you. I want us to all stand together." He began to sink once more into the loveseat. He grabbed at David again to stop the slide. "But this 'work,' you talk about... What 'work' would that be, exactly? I mean to say, what is your ultimate goal? And how is it going to be served by--"

"You want to live under shree-ah law, Reverend?" Blaney snarled. He uncrossed his legs and his boot whumped heavily onto the floor, rattling the pens in a cup on the desk. "You want to see folks beheaded down here on the courthouse square for loving Jesus?"

Brother Birdsong looked at Blaney for a moment, eyes wide. "Well, no," he said quietly, "I certainly wouldn't want to see that." He slowly turned back to Reverend Dumond, though keeping one eye semi-cocked in Blaney's direction. He cleared his throat and went on. "Have you visited with the people at the Center at all? I mean to say, have you *talked* to them?"

"Talk!" barked Blaney, in the manner one might utter a different four-letter word after smacking one's thumb with a hammer.

"I have," said Deion, leaning and twisting to see the Reverend around his wife. "That fellow Berry, or Barry..."

"Dr. Bahri?" said Brother Birdsong. "You've met him?"

"Uh..." Deion's eyes darted back and forth between Blaney and Dumond. He now seemed to regret speaking up. "Just on the phone. He called me. A while back he called and asked if we might be interested in doing a show where we had some of his people on to, you know... Question and answer kind of thing. Learn about each other's... Kind of thing."

"That sounds interesting," said Brother Birdsong.

"I told him I would get back to him," said Deion. "But..."

"Here's where we stand on this, *Bird-song,*" said Blaney impatiently. "We've seen what happens when these people get a foothold. Look at your Germany. Look at your France. And we sure as shit ain't gonna stand for it here."

"All right, Rolly," said Reverend Dumond, raising a hand.

"If anybody is gonna get *be*-headed," Blaney went on angrily, "I want to make damn sure the right heads get...*beed.*" The room was silent as everyone parsed that.

"Well," said Reverend Dumond finally, "maybe Rolly is a little blunt. But the basic facts are as he says. We want to make it clear that we are a Christian country, that these ideas and beliefs are foreign and antithetical to our way of life, and that the people of Boyd County, Tennessee oppose their inculcation into our culture."

"Them words big enough for you?" asked Blaney, still scowling at Brother Birdsong.

"In any case," Reverend Dumond went on, "the decision has been made. This meeting is to discuss the TV program we'll be doing from The Great Rock tonight, and logistics for the action in the morning. If you don't choose to take part, then..." He spread his hands and shrugged. "I'm sorry for the misunderstanding and for wasting your time."

Brother Birdsong tried desperately to rise with some dignity, but given the furniture situation, that wasn't going to happen. After watching a few seconds of his struggle, David stood, took the minister's hand, and heaved him to his feet. "Thank you," said Brother Birdsong, tucking in his shirt tail. He turned to Reverend Dumond. "I'm sorry, too, Raymond," he said. "But the fact is, I guess I *will* be taking part. I'll just be on the other side." He nodded his goodbyes to the couple on the loveseat, said, "Mr. Blaney," and walked out of the office.

"Well that's a hell of a deal," said Rolly Blaney with disgust. "Ain't that a hell of a deal?" He looked around at everyone for confirmation of what kind of a deal that was. "Hell of a deal," he said.

Dumond shrugged, stood, and made his way around to the chair behind the desk. "Losing Birdsong," he said, "doesn't necessarily mean we've lost First Baptist. His congregation may still show up."

"Yeah," chuckled Blaney, "*Both* of 'em."

"Same thing goes for the Methodists and the Nazarenes. Their ministers might lack the intestinal fortitude to stand with us openly, but I'm sure a lot of their people will."

"OK," said Blaney. "Let's get down to tacks here, if the *kum-bah-yah* bullshit is over."

"Language, please, Rolly," said Reverend Dumond with a look of amused disapproval. "There's a lady present." Blaney looked at Mary Mullins doubtfully.

Reverend Dumond said they would be going live from the Great Rock at 7 p.m. to publicize the next morning's gathering at the Islamic Center. The lineup would be headed by Reverend Dumond himself, of course, and would include the local state representative who would explain the bill he was putting forward to protect religious freedom by banning certain unacceptable forms of religious expression. There would also be appearances by some of the popular "stars" from Channel 38. Deion mentioned using the church buses to get people to the site the next morning. Rolly Blaney said something about bikers to escort the buses, but Reverend Dumond deemed that a bit too showy. David paid no attention to any of it. He stared at the empty doorway through which Brother Birdsong had just exited. He had always been able to talk to Brother Birdsong. But, he considered, things were more complicated now. David and Glenda had been members of First Baptist for many years before shifting to the Great Rock. The shift had not been entirely amicable. It had felt to David and, he feared, to Brother Birdsong as well, though he would never show it, that their slipping figuratively away under the cover of metaphorical darkness was a kind of betrayal. Plus, thanks to Glenda, they had taken several other parishioners with them.

"What about you and Glenda?"

Yes, thought David. *Obviously. That's what I want to talk to— Wait a minute. What?*

Everyone was looking at him. He tried to speak and once more only croaked painfully. He coughed. "I'm sorry," he said. "What?"

"What the hell's the matter with you, Burkitt?" Blaney said.

"What are you and Glenda going to do?" said Mary.

"Do?" said David.

"On the show tonight."

"Show?"

"Why the hell do you think you're here?" said Blaney.

David blinked. Of course. The show to rally people to come tomorrow to Keep Tennessee Safe for Christianity. He and Glenda had discussed doing an old Andre Crouch song. He'd been practicing it on guitar. Panic began to rise up in him. "We might... We might not..." He felt his throat begin to close up, possibly for good this time. His face turned red. All those eyes on him. All those people waiting for an explanation.

"I'm not sure we can make it," he choked.

"Not make it?" said Deion. "But..."

"What about tomorrow?" asked Mary. "She's supposed to sing the National Anthem."

"What's the matter?" said Blaney, "Glenda got the trots, too?" He shifted around in his chair to face David and peered at him closely. "Where the hell *is* Glenda, anyway?"

"Let's get back on track," said Reverend Dumond. He rapped on the desk to get their attention. David looked at him with deep gratitude, for changing the subject and for giving him a reason to turn away from Blaney's suspicious glare. "Now, as to the morning's timetable..." Reverend Dumond began going over the schedule, making notes on a pad in front of him, and David once more stopped listening, hearing only the sort of hissing whistle growing in volume inside his head. After a few moments he stood up. "Sorry, I have to go," he said, and stumbled toward the door.

Blaney watched him intently. "Kaopectate, Burkitt," he said.

"I will," said David. "I mean, I—"

"Tell Glenda we said get better," said Mary. David looked at her blankly for a moment, turned, bolted out the door and down the hallway. Laura turned and gave him a strange look as he hurried past her desk, but Laura never gave him any other kind. Mercifully, as he left the building, he encountered no one else asking questions. He found his car, got in and headed for First Baptist Church.

6

The full text of the note that David Burkitt found on his kitchen table under the cat and the Coke machine was, on the positive side, at least short enough to easily consign to memory, which David had done, so now he could run through it in his mind over and over again as he drove blindly through town ignoring stop signs and crosswalks.

The note ran thusly:

Dear David. I am very sorry to hurt you this way but I can't go on as we have been going. [David was under the impression that things had been going fine.] *I need some things that you can't give me* [For instance?] *and I can no longer give you what you need.* [He wasn't feeling deprived of anything...except a wife.] *I hope that someday you will understand.* [Unlikely without some more specific information than that presented thus far.] *Don't look for me, and when you see me, please try to forgive.* [The "when you see me" sounded hopeful, yet the rest was distinctly ominous.] *Goodbye. Glenda.*

Goodbye. Glenda.

Pretty terse, given the plane-crash level of life dislocation the note portended. In between repeating and then interrogating (*Things I can't give you... What specifically?*) the lines in the note, he played back in flashes and snippets his relationship with Glenda, looking for any warning bells, flashing lights or smoking engines that might have predicted this shocking turn of events. But this resembled less a maintenance failure or mechanical malfunction than a full-speed flight into a fog-shrouded mountainside.

Indifference to speed limits and traffic lights got him to First Baptist Church only moments behind Brother Birdsong, who had his hand on the church door as David veered into the parking lot, coming to a stop in one of the angled parking spaces at a completely incorrect angle. The preacher looked surprised, then pleased as David stumbled from the car and approached him. "Well, hello again, David," he said.

Brother Birdsong was an unassuming man, slight in his frame and quiet in his manner, with thinning blond hair and soft gray eyes. David always felt that, in some vague way, he more resembled a professor than a preacher. He had always liked Brother Birdsong, though admittedly his sermons could tend to be on the subtle side, sometimes veering into the didactic. David was a King James man, but Reverend Birdsong, who had gone to a university in addition to a seminary, could and often did read the Bible in the original Greek and Hebrew. He had the unfortunate (some felt) tendency to sometimes stray from the point of the content of scripture into fascinating—to him, anyway—textual analysis. He occasionally even used the word "exegesis," which some parishioners found hard to forgive. But he was generally proficient in the kinds of things that endear a minister to his flock. He visited the sick and the elderly. He comforted the bereaved. He had the ability, somewhat rare in a clergyman, to shut up and listen.

Nevertheless, not everyone found him endearing. When he did stick to the moral implications of scripture, he could sometimes harp on the teachings of Jesus in the context of our various failures to live up to them in our daily interactions and transactions, which made many people antsy. He was prone to emphasizing the beam in one's own eye when a lot of folks really kind of preferred to hear about the motes in other people's. He had recently begun to find himself more and more out of step with many in his church family. For one thing, he steered clear of politics. And while some thought he was too forward-thinking in some ways, others found him simultaneously too conservative in others. For example, he encouraged women to take the lead in many activities traditionally handled by men, but also resolutely refused to allow drums or electric guitars in the sanctuary. There had been some loud controversy and more than a few defections over his announcement that firearms were not welcome inside First Baptist.

Many of those defections had been to The Great Rock Church. While David had always liked Brother Birdsong and still did, Glenda had soured on him. She was the one who insisted on leaving First Baptist for The Great Rock. The Great Rock was cutting edge, plugged into the zeitgeist. Drums, electric guitars and, indeed, firearms were prominent parts of the Great Rock experience, which was also broadcast on all of Dumond's TV stations and streamed on the internet. Jeremy was the lone technician at Channel 38, but the Great Rock church itself had a whole media department. As First Baptist's congregation, once by far the largest in town, had shrunk, the Great Rock, which had started out in a dead Sterling's storefront downtown, had grown. By now it was a holy powerhouse occupying a huge, new, hangar-like building out by the interstate, a rural Hagia Sophia, sans the minarets.

"Brother Birdsong!" said David, hurrying up to him under the portico, "Can I talk to you?"

"Certainly, David. Is it about this protest business? Because I just..."

"No, no!" David shook his head emphatically. "It's uh...personal."

Brother Birdsong looked concerned. "My goodness. I noticed you didn't look too good this morning. What's the matter?"

David found that he was literally unable to say it. Once he said it out loud it would be real, and he did not want it to be real. Brother Birdsong stood quietly and patiently, and his soothing expression ever-so-slightly eased David's anxiety. Finally, David looked at a point in the sky over Brother Birdsong's head, took a deep breath and said, "It's Glenda."

Brother Birdsong said, "Ah."

Spoken human language is a subtle and complex thing. On the page, "Ah" does not seem to amount to much. But with tone in combination with facial expressions and body language, this humble vowel sound can contain a truly astonishing amount of information and subtle nuance. It can convey surprise or sympathy. But it can also, and in this case did, convey instantaneous comprehension, as in, "I already know where this is going," along with, "This information falls into place with other information which I already possess," all beneath a light veneer of, "I have actually long expected to eventually hear something along these lines."

This was certainly not the reaction David was prepared for. It was not even the *vowel* he was prepared for. He was prepared for "oh." Or possibly "oh" with a consonant and an exclamation point, as in, "No!" As for expressions and body language, David was steeled to endure a shooting up of eyebrows, a half-step taken backward, maybe, or a hand rising to cover the mouth. Instead, he got this multifaceted "ah" and a sad head shake and a hand gently squeezing his bicep.

"Let's go into the office," said Brother Birdsong, and he turned and opened the church door.

They walked through the hushed sanctuary, dappled with color from the stained-glass windows. David looked around wistfully. He had always loved this old building. The dark, burnished wood of the pews. The floral curlicues in the plaster on the ceiling. The quiet. Especially the quiet. One thing about The Great Rock: It was never quiet. It constantly blared with one sound or another, or all at once, and all sounded strongly electronically amplified, even the roar of the air conditioning.

They turned right at the pulpit and went through the door next to the organ. Back there was a hallway that led to the Sunday School rooms and offices. In one of these Brother Birdsong's church secretary, who was also the church organist, and who was also Mrs. Birdsong, looked up from a legal pad. "How did it go?" she asked.

"About like you'd expect," said Brother Birdsong with a shrug. "David Burkitt is here. I'm gonna chat with him a while."

Mrs. Birdsong brightened as David looked into the room. She was a pleasant-looking woman in much the same way Brother Birdsong was a pleasant-looking man. She was wearing a blue blouse with white polka dots and had a matching scarf wrapped around her light brown hair. "Hello, David!" she said brightly. "Good to see you! Haven't seen you in forever! How's Glenda?"

"We'll just be a few minutes," Brother Birdsong interjected quickly, and that miracle of tone and body language once more kicked in, working especially efficiently between two people as well-attuned as Brother and Mrs. Birdsong. Despite Brother Birdsong's words being devoid of any situational information, she nodded as if the entire situation had been laid out before her with illustrations and footnotes. David was astonished. Brother Birdsong moved on to the next doorway, and David shuffled after him.

The office was small and unassuming, with one window and a desk that obviously had a lot of miles on it. One wall was lined with bookshelves, which overflowed into stacks on the floor. There were two chairs in front of the desk, and after closing the door Brother Birdsong pulled one around and sat down, pointing to the other. David sat and the two were knee-to-knee. "Tell me about it," said Brother Birdsong.

David found himself once more extremely reluctant to do so. He could not return Brother Birdsong's sympathetic gaze, so he once more chose a spot over the pastor's head, and found himself staring at a piece of paper taped to the bookshelf. It was a crayon drawing in mostly browns and bright greens. A scene crowded with green ovals and brown rectangles, the rectangles seeming to emanate from some silver device in the lower right corner. A smiling bearded man occupied the center, his arms outstretched. David stared at the drawing so long that Brother Birdsong finally turned to see what he was looking at.

"Oh! One of the Sunday School children drew that for me," he said, and turned back around. "It's the Miracle of the Loaves and Fishes." He smiled. "See the silver box there in the corner? Jesus is using a toaster."

"Uh huh," said David. "I see it now." Still looking at the drawing, he reached into his pocket, pulled out the crumpled note and handed it to Brother Birdsong. "Toaster. Yeah. That's cute." Brother Birdsong read the note and sighed. "But if the loaves are toasted," David went on, "shouldn't the fishes be cooked, too? They're just kind of flying around." David pointed at the drawing and twirled his finger. He looked at Brother Birdsong. "Or was it a sort of sushi situation?"

"You found this today?" asked Brother Birdsong.

"Yes. It was under the cat. Partially. Partially under the cat."

"And you don't know where she might have gone, or..." Brother Birdsong trailed off, but again the linguistic subtlety got through. There was a very important part of the sentence which Brother Birdsong had almost said, but then refrained from saying, but David heard it anyway. Did he know where she'd gone...

...Or who with?

Until that moment this idea had not occurred to David at all. Thunderstruck enough by the basic concept, *Glenda Has Left Me*, his mind had never approached the extended concept, ... *for Somebody Else*. He never considered that maybe Glenda, in the midst of saying some things (*I need things that you can't give me*) had, like Brother Birdsong, refrained from saying other things.

...but I know somebody who can.

"I thought maybe, you know," he stammered, "maybe she went to her mom and dad's house. Or something." He hadn't actually thought that, but the possibility at least existed.

"Have you called them?" said Brother Birdsong.

"Uh... No." He had very briefly considered calling them, but he knew somehow that she wouldn't be there. And then they would want to know why he was calling. *Well, it's like this...there were* things, *apparently. Things that I was not able to give her.* "This is right out of the blue, Brother Birdsong," he said, his voice cracking. "Right out of the blue."

Brother Birdsong sat still and looked at him for a long moment before nodding and looking back down at the note. *Now* what was he not saying? David was starting to become a little put out with all this subtlety and unspokenness. He reached out and snatched the paper back from Brother Birdsong's hands, a bit more violently than he intended, and jammed it back into his pocket. "Well," he said testily, "It was!"

"I know! I know!" said Brother Birdsong, patting David on the knee. "Must be a terrible shock. I can't even imagine."

Then why, David wondered, did Brother Birdsong not seem shocked? Shouldn't he be? Maybe not as shocked as David himself was, but at least a little? The minister was acting almost as if David Burkitt's wife up and walking out on him was the most natural thing in the world. "You seem," David began, then halted. "You don't seem..."

There was a light rap on the door, and it opened. Mrs. Birdsong stuck her head into the room. "I'm sorry to interrupt," she said. "I thought maybe you could use a cup of tea." She pushed the door open further, revealing a tray she carried with two cups and a small, Japanese-looking teapot.

Brother Birdsong looked relieved. "Yes, some tea would be nice. Wouldn't it, David? Thank you, dear." He rose and took the tray from Mrs. Birdsong. They traded another of those fraught-with-meaning looks, Mrs. Birdsong patted David on the shoulder, and she went out, softly closing the door behind her.

"Looky here, Brother Birdsong," said David, and stopped. *Did I just say "looky here?"* He started over. "Maybe it's me. It's probably me. I mean, I'm sure it's probably me, but things seem to be... You seem to be..." He cleared his throat, but the problem he was having with words did not originate in his throat. "Something is not right." He gave a coughing little laugh at his own understatement. "You act like you think she...ran off with somebody." There. He said it.

Brother Birdsong looked mournful. "Well, now," he said, and turned to set the tray down on a corner of his desk, shoving some papers aside to make room, turned back and looked David in the eye. "You've seen nothing at all...unusual about Glenda's behavior? Lately? Or...ever?"

"What do you mean, 'unusual?' Ever? What are you talking about?"

Brother Birdsong gave a tiny sigh, reached for the teapot, and began to pour into the two cups. "All right, David. I want you to listen to me. Will you listen to me?"

"Sure," said David. He took the cup Brother Birdsong offered him, blew on it automatically, then forgot he was holding it.

Brother Birdsong set his own cup back on the tray. He looked very serious, which was frightening. "David," he said, "you are a good man."

"Thank you. Nice of you to..." He trailed off.

"And I know for a fact that you have been a good husband."

"Well, I've tried to be." *...some things you can't give me.*

"This time you are going through will be a trial. No doubt about it. And right now I think you're a little in shock. But you must believe me when I say that, though this will definitely be a trial...in the end...it will be for the best."

David twitched and the tea swirled in his cup. "For the best?" he cried. "What do you mean, for the best?"

"Now David, listen to me. This is hard, I know. It's hard for me, too, believe me. But I feel like I have to say this. There are some things that you haven't been aware of."

"Things?" His cup began to rattle in its saucer.

"Yes." Brother Birdsong squirmed a bit in his chair.

"Things," David repeated. "O.K. I see." He didn't. Whatever he expected when he chased down Brother Birdsong to consult with him, this, whatever the heck it was, was not it. He wanted to hear something helpful. He didn't want to hear about *things*. He raised his gaze from the minister's pained expression and looked once more at the crayon drawing on the bookcase. Jesus. Loaves and fishes. A toaster. Very cute.

Keep Calm and Trust Jesus.

"Thank you for your time, Brother Birdsong!" David blurted, and he jumped to his feet. "I better be going." He reached for the door, saw to his surprise that he had a teacup in his hand, and swiveled back to drop it messily onto the tray. Brother Birdsong also stood. "Wait a minute, David!"

David clawed the door open and bounced out into the hall. "I'd like to stay, but I gotta be going. We have a show tonight. The song has barre chords."

"Please don't go yet, David!" Brother Birdsong tried to take David's arm, but he snatched it away. He started down the hallway in a brisk walk that changed to a sprint as he approached the doorway. "Thank you for your help!" he shouted back over his shoulder. The door to the sanctuary flew back with a bang.

"David!" Brother Birdsong called after him, but he was gone. Mrs. Birdsong stepped into the hallway and looked at the slowly closing door. "Poor man," she said, and the two shared another look, this one the most fraught of all.

David drove over two curbs and a grassy verge on his way to getting his car more or less into the street. He headed automatically toward home. There wasn't anywhere else to go. He wanted to look for Glenda but had no idea where to even start. Brother Birdsong's cryptic references and meaningful glances had completely unnerved him. He drifted into the other lane and an oncoming car had to move nearly off the road to avoid him. The car's horn blared. "Sorry!" David said to the rearview mirror. He shook his head to clear it, which didn't work, and gripped the steering wheel more tightly, the car weaving slightly in consequence. What was there which would make Brother Birdsong suggest that this disaster might be "for the best?" It was all crazy. Granted, lately it did sometimes seem that Glenda was off doing her volunteer work and club meetings and TV show post-production a lot. Sometimes it seemed she was gone more than she was home. But she was a woman who liked to keep busy! And when she was home she had been spending more and more time hunching over the keyboard of the computer in her corner off the dining room, communicating with people on the internet. But that was just her hobby.

Coca-Cola memorabilia.

7

The entire world seemed to have shifted, David thought as he pulled into his driveway. The light seemed different. The air felt odd. Existence itself was now subtly askew. His house was the same house, but it now looked different somehow. Off kilter. Out of true. He dreaded entering it. He sat in his car for several minutes before forcing himself to get out and go to the front door. Once in the living room, he went immediately to the bookshelf on the left-hand wall and pulled out a Bible. The red one with his and Glenda's names embossed on the cover in gold. The one his parents had given them when they were married. He turned and looked at the living room. The disjointed feeling continued. The place felt different. It even smelled different. It smelled like...

Cigarettes?

He took a step toward the entryway from the living room to the kitchen and dining room and was brought up short. Bitsy the cat crouched just inside the doorway. She was looking into the dining area, ears laid flat and the hair on her back standing up. She darted a look at David, gave a dreadful spitting hiss at something around the corner out of David's view, and took off, her feet slipping in place on the tile floor like a Tom and Jerry cartoon before she caught the living room carpet and shot like a missile down the hallway toward the bedrooms.

David listened but heard nothing. He began a slow creep toward the kitchen doorway. He tried to stay silent but clunked against the coffee table. Should he try to find some sort of weapon? There was nothing in the room that could be used as one with the possible exception of a hat tree by the front door. The thought of charging into the kitchen with a hat rack was absurd. He looked at the Bible in his hands. Useful, maybe, if there was a demon in his kitchen, or a vampire, but those probably didn't smoke cigarettes. He laid the Bible on the coffee table and moved forward empty-handed. He reached the doorway and slowly peeped around the corner.

At the kitchen table, legs crossed, smoking a cigarette, sat Rolly Blaney. "I don't know why the hell anybody would keep a goddamn cat in their house," he said. "They make rat poison now, you know."

David had already been stunned several times that day, but this was an undiscovered species of stunned. The fact that things just kept out-stunning one another was stunning in its own right. He was no more prepared to find Rolly Blaney in his kitchen than he would have been to find a vampire or a demon. "Wha?" he said.

Blaney mashed his cigarette out in a Coca-Cola-themed ashtray on the table. David recognized it as an ashtray that belonged on a shelf next to the refrigerator. It wasn't supposed to actually be used, and if it *was* used, certainly not as an ashtray! Glenda would be-- David's mouth snapped shut, then opened again to say, "Mr. Blaney?" He sounded as though he doubted it, which he did.

Blaney squinted at him for a moment through the last wisps of cigarette smoke. "Where you been?" he asked.

"I was..." David pointed over his shoulder. "I just came..." He closed his eyes for a moment to collect himself. Why should he be the one answering questions? "What's going on? What are you doing here?"

Blaney ignored the question, continued to squint at him. "You was acting awful funny at that meeting, Burkitt," he said.

"Meeting?" David moved into the room, drifting toward the kitchen counter, mainly because he felt the need to lean against something. *What meeting? Oh, that meeting.* It already seemed im-possibly long ago. "I wasn't... Funny? What do you mean?"

"What I said. What I say is always what I mean."

What did *that* mean? David looked at the sink, suddenly desiring a drink of water. "Look here, Mr. Blaney," he said, annoyed at the shakiness behind his voice, but happy that he at least hadn't said *looky* here, "you can't just--"

"You was acting awful funny," Blaney repeated, "and I couldn't help noticing that every time somebody asked you where Glenda was, you never would answer. And now I come over here and," he raised his hands in a sweeping gesture, "no Glenda."

"Well! Well," David stammered, "Glenda isn't here. Right now."

"I just said that," said Blaney. He tilted his head, an oddly doglike gesture. "You act halfway like you're on something, Burkitt. You on something, Burkitt?"

"On something? Of course I'm not on something! Anything."

"Uh huh." Blaney stood up, still squinting, and ambled across the room, his eyes never leaving David. "Well, something sure has got you all balled up."

"Balled?" David said. "I'm not.... I don't think I'm..." He sputtered out.

Blaney reached the window and turned to pull aside the curtain and look out into the back yard. For the first time David noticed that Blaney had a holster on his belt. It held a large, black pistol. Blaney pressed close to the glass and looked both ways into the yard as far as he could. He spoke again without turning around, his voice now casual, almost friendly.

"Nice yard out there."

David had no rational response to that non sequitur.

"Flower bed," Blaney said, tapping a finger on the windowpane. "When did you put that in?" He turned and looked at David once more. "Looks recent."

Oh, I see, David thought wildly. *He just dropped by to discuss landscaping and horticulture.* "What?" he said, "What?" David felt his throat closing up again.

Blaney maintained his dead-eyed stare, and David simply couldn't stand up to it. He jerked around, yanked open a cabinet, snatched out a glass and turned to the sink. He had to have that drink of water. "Why is everybody asking about flowerbeds?" he said plaintively, then shook his head sharply. "I mean Glenda. Why is everybody asking about Glenda?" He then tried to give a nonchalant laugh, but it came off as more of a gag.

Blaney slowly moved closer.

"Here's the thing," Blaney said, his voice low and cold. "Since you ask. Seems like nobody has heard from her. She don't reply to texts. Her phone goes to mail. She don't answer email and she ain't on the Facebook." David took a step back, the glass of water in hand. Blaney was too close now. David could smell his cigarette breath along with a strange chemical scent he could not identify. "So I'm gonna ask you something, Burkitt. All right if I ask you something?"

David felt water from the glass splash out onto his fingers. "O.K.," he said warily.

Blaney shifted his weight to his left leg and laid one hand on the butt of his pistol. He gave another of those Clint Eastwood squints. Then he said the most stunning thing yet.

"What did you do to her?"

For much of the morning David's mind had been experiencing a processing backlog. A crowd of disorienting circumstances were clamoring to be puzzled out, all trying to shove through his mind's doorway at the same time. There were so many bizarre occurrences requiring deep consideration that they had formed a mental logjam. There was the overarching puzzle of what in the world possessed Glenda to leave, but there was also Brother Birdsong's inexplicable reaction, or lack thereof, to the news of her leaving. There was the distraction of being called upon to save Christianity. Now the unanticipated, *unanticipatable* appearance of Rolly Blaney in his kitchen, was followed by the information that for some reason Blaney, whom he barely knew and whom until very recently he would have said Glenda didn't know at all, not only knew her, but apparently had her phone number and email address. For a few brief seconds Blaney's question couldn't break through the crowd or rise above the din. When it did, David shook his head like a wet dog and dropped his glass of water to the countertop, where it fell over and spilled across the formica.

"What did *who* to *what*?" he yelled.

Blaney flinched, but not quite enough to cause him to draw his weapon. "You heard me," he said, but there was a tiny feather of uncertainty in his voice.

"You're asking me if I *did something* to Glenda?" David's astonishment shoved aside every other feeling—anger at being confronted in his own kitchen, puzzlement at Blaney's familiarity with his wife, even his dismay at Glenda's leaving. Someone thought he, David Burkitt, had "done something" to her? Him? To Glenda?

"Me?" he cried. "To Glenda? Are you completely out of your mind?"

Now David took a step forward and it was Blaney's turn to back away. Blaney had presumably expected a denial, even an angry denial, but he hadn't expected one that sounded so sincere. "Well," he said somewhat doubtfully, "did you?"

David took another step, and Blaney continued to retreat before the shockwave of righteous indignation. "How could you even ask such a thing? Do something to Glenda? I could never 'do anything' to Glenda!" He threw up his hands. "And why would I?"

Blaney gave once more that doglike tilt of his head. "You serious?" he said.

"O.K.," David half shouted. "Excuse me!" He sidestepped Blaney and strode to the table. He snatched up the ashtray and dumped its contents into the trash container at the end of the counter. He thrust the ashtray under the faucet and rinsed it out, set it on the drain board next to the sink, picked up the water glass and set it next to the ashtray. He wheeled around. He reached into his pocket and yanked out the fatal note, now tattered as well as crumpled, and thrust it toward Blaney. "Here! Go ahead! Everybody seems to know things I don't, so why not know it all?"

Blaney took the note. David went to the chair Blaney had sat in and collapsed onto it. Blaney read through the note and looked at David, his hostility now dissipated. He walked over, pulled out another chair and sat down. He tossed the note onto the table. "That's a hell of a deal," he said.

"Yes, it is," said David wearily.

They sat in silence for a moment, then Blaney said, "You got anything to drink around here?"

David could tell from his tone that he wasn't referring to soft drinks. "We don't drink," he said.

"You mean *you* don't," said Blaney.

"What? What do you--"

"All this Coke," Blaney said irritably, waving a hand around at the room, "and no whiskey?"

"No!" said David. "No whiskey! Mr. Blaney, just what exactly are you even doing—"

"Stop calling me 'mister,' goddamn it!" Blaney slammed a hand down onto the table and raised it up again clutching the crumpled note. "What are you gonna do about this, Burkitt?"

That, David realized, though he could not fathom why it was Rolly Blaney asking it, was actually a good question. He considered it for a moment. He had been flailing around in a fog. Sooner or later he would have to actually decide what to do. But what was there to be done? What *could* he do?

"What *can* I do?" he said.

"Are you shitting me?" Blaney said. "Some asshole steals your wife, and you're gonna what? Do *nothing*?"

David pointed at the note. "It doesn't actually say anything about there being another—"

"Jesus H. Christ!' Blaney slammed the note back down onto the table, and David recoiled, from the gesture and from the words. No one had ever taken that name in vain in his house before. "You need to wake up and smell the coffee!" Blaney stood and hitched up his belt, sliding his holster into place. He looked around the room as though searching for something to shoot.

Wake up and smell the coffee, David thought. Yes. How nice it would be to wake up and smell the coffee! The coffee in his kitchen, where he would find his wife waiting for him, not some raving red-neck. *Good morning, sweetheart. Good morning, dear. How did you sleep? Not too well, actually. I had this awful, awful nightmare...*

Blaney turned back to David. "Where's the computer? She's got a computer. Did she take it with her?"

"Hm?" *All just a dream. A terrible, terrible—*

"Hey! The computer, goddammit!"

David goggled at him for a moment before pointing to the door to the laundry room. "It's in there. But what--"

Blaney strode across the floor and through the door. David looked down at the crumpled, tattered note. He picked it up and put it back in his pocket. *A nightmare,* he thought.

"Burkitt!" Blaney shouted from the next room, "Does she back her phone up in the cloud?"

What her what in the what? "What?" David said. Rolly Blaney was in his laundry room. It was definitely a nightmare, but sadly it wasn't a dream.

"Never mind!" Blaney muttered several presumably obscenities, then shouted, "She's cleared her browser history. Does she always do that?"

"I don't know what you're–" David began.

"I don't recognize this email account. How many does she have?" This question was apparently also rhetorical, as he went on, "What's her password?" This one was not rhetorical, since after a two-second pause Blaney shouted, "You hear me? Her Gmail!"

David couldn't follow. "Her what?"

Blaney appeared in the doorway. "Damn it, Burkitt! Get your head in the game!" He pointed back into the room toward the computer. "Her email password. What is it?"

All these bizarre questions! David shrugged. "I don't know."

Blaney shook his head in disgust. "What kind of pussy-whipped asshole don't know his wife's email password?"

David stood up, anger finally overcoming inertia. "Here now!"

Blaney's looked at him in disbelief. "'*Here now?*' Somebody calls you a pussy-whipped asshole, and you say '*Here now?*'"

"Sorry!" David snapped. "I'm not used to being cursed at. In my own house! By somebody who broke in!"

Blaney waved a hand dismissively. "Door was unlocked." He leaned on the doorframe, his attention already elsewhere. "Looks like she's wiped the damn thing, except for her Gmail login." He sighed in frustration and looked around the room. Then he looked around again more slowly. "Wait a minute," he said, and disappeared back into the laundry room.

David followed him. Blaney was sitting at Glenda's computer. He had brought up the log-in page for the email program. "What do you think you're doing?"

"What you oughta done already," said Blaney, typing. He hit "enter" and got an incorrect password warning. "Shit! Gotta get this in a couple of tries or it'll lock me out."

"Just a minute," said David. "You have no right—"

"Shut up," said Blaney, poking at the keys. Enter. Another error message. "Shit!"

"This is an invasion of privacy!" said David.

Blaney ignored him. He grabbed the mouse and in a couple of clicks brought up a search page. In the search box he typed, "Coca-Cola advertising slogan." He paused, clicked again and added "first" before the word "advertising." Several links popped up and Blaney squinted at them. He nodded, reopened the email screen and typed again. "Drink," he said, "Coca-Cola." He paused, considered. "Exclamation point." He gave the enter key a solid jab.

"Wah-lah," Blaney said as an email inbox appeared on the screen.

8

Among the fragments of memory and flashbacks to better days that David would be experiencing over the next twenty-four hours, one was himself standing in the control room at Channel 38 a few minutes before he and Glenda began their first broadcast. He was nervous, of course. He had never been on television before. Other than playing guitar in the common room back at the BSU or leading a prayer at First Baptist he had never really "performed" in front of people at all. The TV program was Glenda's idea, and it had taken a while to convince him. What would they talk about? Who would watch? What if he played the wrong chord when accompanying her on guitar? But her unshakeable confidence won him over. Not that there was any doubt, really. He always went along with Glenda's ideas in the end. She was seldom wrong.

On one of the monitors on the control room wall was the program on the air at the moment, the show that would be leading into theirs. It was a taped program featuring a preacher from Kentucky named Hiram Goble. He was a large, red-faced man, and at the moment he was speaking in a highly animated manner while standing with a stick in his hand next to an easel holding a colorful map of the Middle East, coming dangerously close to knocking the whole thing over by occasionally using the stick to punctuate a point. The audio was turned low, but Goble's voice could still be heard, as though no amount of electronic attenuation could completely conquer his heroic volume. "Meggido!" Goble's small voice shouted, and he thwacked the map. The little needles on the audio board clicked against the right sides of their meters.

Jeremy the Chief Engineer, whom David at that point had only recently met, sat at the video board with his headset on. David wasn't certain what the headset was for, as there were no camera operators for him to direct, the three cameras in the studio being locked in place on their two close-ups and a wide shot. Jeremy didn't speak to them through the headset; he spoke to them in the studio, when that was called for, via a microphone on a flexible stalk which he activated with a switch on his console. Maybe the headset was just to keep his ears warm; it was quite chilly in there, and he wore no jacket. Glenda was out in the studio on their set, which consisted of two chairs, a fake potted plant with his guitar next to it on a stand, and a background of white lattice hung with fake ivy.

"That Glenda," said Jeremy, leaning back in his chair and rubbing his arms, "she's a natural. I mean it. Camera presence, you know?" Jeremy's t-shirt featured the name, "Jesus" with the "J" formed by the swoosh of a sneaker logo, over the words, "Just Believe It."

David looked at his wife on one of the monitors, her expression passive as she looked over her notes for the show, which they had agreed would be on the topic of The Christian Foundations of a Successful Marriage. Yes, he thought, the camera did flatter her. Not that she needed any flattery. And she was not nervous in the least, though she had never been on television, either. He felt a wave of love and pride. For her beauty, her talent and her competence. He was a lucky man. "Yes," he said with a chuckle. "That's good for me. Everyone will be looking at her."

Jeremy looked up at him. "Oh," he said blandly, "you'll do alright." It was the least enthusiastic endorsement David had ever heard, and if it was intended to reassure him, it achieved the opposite effect. "Hiram's winding down," said Jeremy.

"Oh! Right." David hurried into the studio and took his place in his chair. He clipped the little microphone onto his shirt as Jeremy had instructed. Looking up, he saw the studio monitor. It showed the two-shot. Himself and Glenda, side by side. The Glenda on the monitor turned to look at him and extended a hand. The television David extended his hand. David watched as Television David and Television Glenda touched one another. Real David felt the warmth on his fingers.

9

"Shit-eating, bristle-faced, pencil-dicked motherfucker!"

Rolly Blaney's nose was inches from the computer screen. He had been clicking and reading for almost a minute, his head snapping left to right, emitting low rumbles and little gagging sounds, as David stood nearby trying to decide how he should be acting right now. He really ought to demand Blaney turn off the computer at once. He was indignant, insulted, offended. But he was also curious. Why hadn't it occurred to him to try to get into Glenda's email? But then, he would never have been able to figure out how. How had Rolly Blaney--

It was at that point that Blaney leaped to his feet, sending his chair flying, and erupted into that cascade of obscenity. David recoiled, clattering into the ironing board hanging on the wall next to the door. "What what what?" he cried. Blaney slammed a fist down onto the computer's keyboard. He turned, his face twisted in fury. "What *what*?" David repeated.

"That little fucker," Blaney growled.

"What little..." David began. "What?"

"That little TV fucker! That half-ass hippy-looking little shit at the TV station!" Blaney shouted, and he shoved past David into the kitchen. David followed.

"TV...person?" There was only one person who came to mind who might fit that description. "You mean Jeremy? What about him?"

Blaney turned and faced David. He put his hands on his hips, his face thrust forward. "What the hell do you *think*?"

At first, David honestly couldn't imagine what he was supposed to think. He had a flash of a bad dream he once had in which he found himself a contestant on *Jeopardy*, a TV show he was quite fond of. The clue in the dream was something he knew he should know. In fact, it was something everyone should know. Everyone *did* know it, and everyone was staring at him, waiting for him to give the obvious correct answer. But he couldn't. He knew he should know it, but he couldn't think of it. Everyone was waiting, and that music was playing. That little theme song. Louder and louder. He heard the song in his head now as the silence stretched out and Blaney scowled at him much as Alex Trebek had in his dream. In his dream, Alex Trebek was still alive.

But of course, he did know this answer. Unlike the dream in which he was unable to call it up, in this case he was simply unwilling. When it elbowed its way into his mind in spite of all he could do to keep it out, he was certainly unwilling to say it. But Blaney nodded at him, indicating that his eyes had betrayed him and had said it in spite of him.

"Yeah," said Blaney. "Yeah."

They stood looking at each other for several seconds, Blaney's jaw clenched, David's hanging slack. The refrigerator kicked on. Somewhere in the house Bitsy gave a mournful meow.

"*Well?*" Blaney shouted. David jumped. The tiny vending machine in the center of the table fell over with a *clunk.*

"I don't believe it!" David said. But details, small, remembered details, came flying at him like arrows out of the darkness. He tried to dodge them but couldn't avoid them all. Chunks of heretofore unregarded knowledge that had been floating aimlessly in his consciousness now began to take on mass and fall into mental slots with almost audible clicks. Glenda spending so much time at the television station. Going down there every Thursday evening. To make promos and to "help with the editing." To help *Jeremy* with the editing.

You seen Glenda? She was gonna meet me last night.

"Jeremy?"

Blaney threw up his hands, turned and began to angrily pace the room. He couldn't fathom it either, apparently.

But, David thought, *but...* "Are you sure you read it right?" he said.

"Read it yourself," said Blaney. "If you want to read about what they done. And where they done it. Shit, I don't know! You might could *watch* it. He might have videos!"

David jerked as if electrocuted.

"Well?" Blaney snapped again. "What are you waiting for?"

"Waiting?" David said.

"Let's go, God dammit!" Blaney strode to the back door and yanked it open.

"Go?" said David.

Blaney stared at him for a moment, released the doorknob and walked toward him. The table scraped on the tile floor as David tried to back away. Blaney stopped inches away and looked into his eyes. Then his hand shot out and grabbed David roughly in the crotch. David gave a loud, very high-pitched screech as Blaney gave his genitals a momentary squeeze before releasing him and stepping back. David clutched himself and bent over.

"Yeah," said Blaney, "they're there. I was beginning to wonder. Now *let's go!*" He grabbed David by the collar and propelled him toward the back door.

10

Blaney had parked his pickup on the back side of their garage, presumably to facilitate his earlier ambush when David came home. He more or less dragged David to it and tossed him in through the driver's side door. "Other door don't work," Blaney said, climbing in himself and shoving David to the far side of the seat. He tore deep, ragged ruts in David's lawn getting back out into the street, where he left a sixty-foot double line of burned rubber on the pavement. David reached automatically for a seatbelt, only to find that this truck had none. He settled for bracing himself with both hands against the dashboard and pressing his feet into the floorboard. He was flung sideways on the seat at every right turn and slammed against the door at every left. Blaney drove hunched over the steering wheel, feet stamping the brake and clutch like an Irish dancer while his arm worked the shifter on the steering column like a manic gambler at a slot machine, all the while muttering obscenities.

In spite of all the terror and repeated blows to the head against the side window, David somehow managed to think. He remembered the startling encounter with Jeremy in the hallway earlier that day. The fuzzy red rectangle. The sudden appearance. *Hey, Dave! You seen Glenda?*

"It can't be him!" he screamed.

"Wise up, Burkitt!" Blaney leaned on the horn as he swerved around a car irritatingly traveling at the speed limit.

"I saw Jeremy this morning!" David cried. "He asked me where she was! Said he called her and she didn't answer! Why would he ask all that if she was with him?"

Blaney looked at him for a moment, then back at the road. He said nothing more until they fishtailed into the parking lot at Channel 38 and skidded to a stop on the sidewalk directly in front of the door. The truck bucked as he popped the clutch and the motor died. Blaney turned in the seat to face David, who was panting, still gripping the dashboard. "What kind of man are you?" he asked.

"I'm– I think I'm just as much— Where do you, you, you—" David babbled.

"Yeah," said Blaney. "That's what I figured. Come on anyway." He yanked the handle on his door and threw his weight against it to send it swinging with a loud, squealing creak, reached over, grabbed David, and dragged him out of the truck.

11

The second most popular program on Channel 38 after David and Glenda's *The Light in Your Life* was *Our Father's Table*, a Christian cooking show presented by Robin Sullivan, high school teacher of Family and Community Sciences, which used to be, and by Mrs. Sullivan still was, called "Home Ec," and Margaret Fletcher, an older lady with no academic credentials, but who was an experienced mother, grandmother and homemaker, as well as, their fans agreed, excellent comedy relief. Their program had even won a regional Christian TV "Jemmy" (they couldn't call it an Emmy for legal reasons) for their episode re-creating their best guess at the likely menu at the Last Supper.

Because of the complications of faking the cooking of meals, *Our Father's Table* was pre-taped, and today was their day. Mrs. Sullivan and Margaret were in the studio at their table covered with cooking paraphernalia. The studio had no functional stove or oven, so they brought the dishes pre-cooked for presentation as a *fait accompli* at the end of the program. Today was an ethnic day. They were demonstrating Mrs. Sullivan's special recipe for something she called "authentic taco casserole."

The production of this show, with its props and manipulation of bowls and utensils, was of such a complexity that it required an actual camera operator–Margaret's 14-year-old grandson, Bobby. Jeremy, as always, was in the control room, enjoying the rare experience of having a crew member to direct, although Bobby was a camera operator who, as often as not and to Jeremy's considerable annoyance, tended to go his own way.

"Camera one," Jeremy said into his headset microphone, which designation being less than crucial, there being only the one manned camera, "Go in close on the lettuce. No, the lettuce." The image on the monitor labeled CAM 1 remained resolutely of the bowl of sour cream.

"Now," Mrs. Sullivan said, "we add the sour cream."

"Yum!" said Margaret.

"Ooh, it's good stuff," Robin agreed, "but if you're watching your calories, you may want to go a little easy on it."

A mere glance at Margaret suggested that she at no time showed much mercy to any type of foodstuff. "Easy on the sour cream?" she squealed. "*No comprendo!*"

The two women cackled at that for a while, and Jeremy cut to the wide shot. "Camera one," he said, "Give me the lettuce. No kidding. The lettuce." Then he felt the headset snatched from his head, the cord wrapped twice around his neck, and his body yanked over backward out of his chair.

In the studio, Margaret's grandson Bobby was panning from the sour cream to the hamburger meat, which was obviously what should be shown next regardless of what the dork with the beard said. But he paused and put a hand to his headset. There was suddenly a lot of noise coming through. Like static...but more like voices. Or rather, not exactly *voices* voices, that is, *human* voices, but more like vaguely *humanoid*, voicelike noises. Groans. Gurgles. In between the inhuman noises the jumbled "voices" seemed to say indistinct words, like some unknown language, or a known one played backwards. He couldn't make it out. It reminded him of the spooky soundtracks of the horror movies he guiltily watched on his phone late at night in his room because his parents wouldn't let him watch them on the television. Just the night before, in fact, he had watched one about a group of teenagers trapped in an abandoned and enthusiastically haunted insane asylum. The evil spirits in that movie had such voices. He knew he really shouldn't watch movies like that. His whole family were members of the Great Rock Church and had all heard Reverend Dumond explain how the forces of Evil wrapped themselves in the cloak of supposedly harmless "entertainments," creating devious lures for unprotected minds, weakening the barriers between our world and that of the Demonic Powers until those powers–the powers of Satan–could come breaking through. Once that happened, alas, it was too late.

Bobby turned and looked toward the control room. The window was elevated slightly, so he could not see directly into the room; plus, it was dark in there. He could see some of the glowing LEDs on the equipment. Shadowy shapes moved about, occluding the lights here and there. He couldn't make out who or what they were. The scuffling, gurgling noises in his headset continued. He looked at his grandmother and Mrs. Sullivan. They hadn't noticed anything. They had moved on to the discussion of the ground beef. Ground chuck, they agreed, cost more, but was less greasy than the cheap stuff.

Bobby turned back toward the control room, heart racing, forgetting about Camera 1, which was now pointing at nothing in particular. He cupped a hand around his headset's microphone and said in his low, cameraman voice, "Hey Jermy? Jermy? You OK?" The demonic voices on his headset went suddenly quiet. He listened for a long moment, then said again, "Jermy? Hello?" There was another moment of pregnant silence, then a rustle, then a clunk. Bobby saw a shadow rise up in the control room and step toward the window, growing larger if no less indistinct. A voice, deep and gravelly, burst shockingly loud in his ears.

"Piss off, you little shit!"

Bobby gave a sharp cry, ripped his headset off and tossed it away. After another terrified look at the shadowy shape in the control room window, he turned and ran across the studio to the door in the back wall, slammed against the bar, knocked it open, shot out into the sunshine and disappeared down the alley, done forever not just with *Our Father's Table,* but also with horror films of any kind, on his phone or anywhere else.

Margaret and Mrs. Sullivan stood, ground chuck in hand, and watched Bobby sprint across in front of them and away. They looked up at the window of the control room, uncertain what exactly they should do. What happened? Were they still recording? Finally, Margaret, in the spirit of "the show must go on," said, "Well! That don't usually happen until *after* they've had the taco casserole!"

12

Blaney dropped the headset and turned from the window. He plopped down onto the video console, which sent the lights on the buttons flashing and the monitors into a paroxysm of blinking and flipping from the puzzled faces of the women in the studio to the bowls on the table and back again. Jeremy lay gasping and coughing on the floor, rubbing his throat. David leaned, enervated, against one of the equipment racks. Desperately trying to convince Blaney that given the need to acquire more information, strangling Jeremy would be counterproductive, had taken a lot out of him.

"What the heck?" Jeremy said. This brought on another fit of coughing. Then, once more, "What the *heck*?"

"All right you pissant," said Blaney, "Where is she?"

"Where's who?" Jeremy choked. "What are you talking about?" He pointed at the console Blaney was sitting on and whined, "We're in the middle of a production. You can't bust in and choke somebody in the middle of a production!"

"You better produce an answer to my question, shitbird."

Jeremy crab-walked backward across the floor on feet and elbows until he reached the wall and used it to shakily stand. He felt his throat. "You choked me!" he said. "Why did you choke me?"

"Keep fucking with me and I'll do it some more." Blaney stood and took a step toward him. "Where's Glenda?"

"Glenda?" Jeremy squeaked. He glanced at David, looked away. "What about Glenda?"

"You heard me! Where is she?"

"How would I know?"

Blaney took another step forward. "Drop that innocent crap. We know what you been up to."

Jeremy's eyes widened and he looked at David again. "Up to? What...?"

"Thursdays. In the edit room." Blaney stalked closer. Jeremy, against the wall already, could retreat no farther. Blaney stopped, his face a foot from Jeremy's. His voice lowered and through clenched teeth he said, "Don't worry, babe. I've got an afghan for the sofa." Jeremy gasped and shot another frightened glance at David.

"What?" David said. "Afghan?"

Blaney spoke to David without taking his eyes off Jeremy. "She had complained, you see. About the couch in there. The vinyl was cold." Jeremy began to quiver. "Yeah. I seen the emails, you little turd. So cut the bullshit."

David stepped forward, brow furrowed. His fingers went to his temples. "Wait a minute. Wait a minute. What couch? What's this about an afghan?" His circuits had just started to quiet down, but now were once more sparking and threatening overload.

Jeremy's eyes darted back and forth between David and Blaney's looming, furious face. "Oh, man," he said sadly.

"Now," said Blaney, "I'll ask you one last time. Where is she?"

"Why do you keep asking me that? I don't know! Last night was..." He paused, swallowed. "But she didn't show up."

"But she did," David said. It came back to him through a fog, like a memory from decades ago. Last night. Last century. "She went out. To her club meeting, and to do the editing."

"But she didn't. She didn't show up. I waited... Look, Dave–" Jeremy extended a hand toward David and made as though to step away from the wall, but Blaney put a hand on his chest and roughly shoved him back. Jeremy yelped. "I'm sorry! I'm sorry! I know it wasn't right. But Glenda... She... She was..." His eyes glazed and he shook his head, but snapped back into the moment again with a twitch. "It just... It just *happened*."

"Happened?" David murmured. *Happened.* He rolled the word around in his mind. *Happened.* What happened? *It* happened. *It.* And the sofa is vinyl. And the vinyl was cold.

Blaney barked a sarcastic laugh. "It just *happened*! Yeah. It just happened. Every Thursday. For how long? Months? Years?"

Jeremy's eyes darted back and forth between the two men. "It wasn't *every* Thursday."

Blaney's left hand lashed out and smacked the wall inches from Jeremy's right ear. Jeremy cowered and cried out. "What's your problem?"

"What?" Blaney shouted.

"You heard me! What are *you* so mad about?" He pointed at David. "She's *his* wife!"

Blaney took a small step back. In the sudden silence the pleasant humming of the various machines became audible. Jeremy, with an air of recovering his dignity, began straightening his t-shirt. David noticed that the image on the shirt was different from the earlier cryptic mustache. This one had an image of a Star Trek-style communicator with a glowing cross emblazoned upon it, beneath the words, "Beam Me Up, Jesus." David contemplated the shirt and repeated the message in his head as an earnest prayer. He waited, listened to the humming in the air, but the prayer, like all the others lately, was not answered. The humming sound began to waver rhythmically, to rise and fall in volume and to shift spatially from near the end of his nose to far away on either side, an interesting effect caused by the fact that the humming in the room was slightly out of phase with the humming inside his head. He felt he was drifting in a void. A rhythmically thrumming void. Surely *this* was a dream. A nightmare. It had to be. He knew that was a cliche, but he couldn't think of anything else that could explain it all. Isn't "this must be a dream" what one would think if, for example, the furniture went into a dance and the potted plant began to sing a Hank Williams tune? That was the level of unreality he was feeling.

Glenda? Jeremy? Vinyl? *Afghan?*

In the looming void he discerned a kernel of light. It was bright. It was unmissable yet, he realized, he had hitherto somehow missed it. For some strange reason he had not perceived it, though he had the feeling it had been there for some time. Maybe it had been in a blind spot. He was beginning to think perhaps he had a lot of blind spots. Maybe whole blind regions. Continents. How would you know, when you're blind to them? Or maybe it was that in the cascade of flashes, the veritable 4th of July fireworks display of blinding revelations, this one flash, despite its seeming prominence in retrospect, had simply been drowned out. It was definitely clear now, though. It flared and burst out blood red.

"Yes," he said, surprised at the calmness of his own voice. "Yes, Mr. Blaney. What *are* you so mad about?"

13

After Bobby fled the demonic voice and Margaret delivered her punchline, the two women stood silently watching the dark control room window, waiting for some indication as to whether they should continue, or stop, or start over, or what. "Are we going to–" Mrs. Sullivan began, but she was interrupted by the *click-squelch* of the intercom coming on. Ah! Good. Jeremy was going to give them some instructions. The intercom had not been engaged by Jeremy's finger however, but by Rolly Blaney's behind when he sat on the control console. Instead of Jeremy's reedy voice, a much deeper voice with a metallic reverberation said, *All right, you pissant. Where is she?*

The ladies looked at one another. *What on Earth?* The voices continued, and it became clear that some sort of altercation was taking place. Mrs. Sullivan set down the bowl of ground chuck. They leaned forward, listening. The voices, though loud, were hollow and difficult to understand. The gist came through, however. They looked at each other, mouths agape, listening like avid fans of a radio soap opera, trading expressions of astonishment and gasps of scandalization at every unforeseen revelation.

When a scratchy voice said, *Yes, Mr. Blaney. What are you so mad about?* the two women leaned even farther forward in anticipation. But at that point, like a soap opera cliffhanger, the voices went silent. There was only the hiss of the speaker. Had the intercom stopped working? If Margaret could have reached the speaker, she would have banged on it. Then the door to the control room swung open and Rolly Blaney stepped into the studio.

Blaney stopped and looked at the women. The women looked back at him. This standoff did not last long before the look in Blaney's eyes caused the women to turn and flee, unhooking their microphones and looking anxiously over their shoulders, out the door leading into the TV station hallway.

Blaney continued into the room. A few moments later David followed, then came Jeremy, still rubbing his throat. Blaney walked jerkily to the table and paced up and down along it, seeming to study the cooking implements and ingredients. David spoke, his voice shaky. "Well? Are you going to answer me?"

Blaney moved to the end of the table where a baking dish sat covered with aluminum foil. This was the finished dish Mrs. Sullivan and Margaret had brought along to reveal at the end of their cooking instructions. Blaney peeled up a corner of the foil and studied the contents disdainfully. "Who the hell," he said, "puts lettuce in a casserole?"

"It's supposed to be like a taco," said Jeremy.

Blaney looked at him. "*What*?"

David stepped between them. "Excuse me?" he snapped. Then, to Blaney: "What is going on here? You break into my house–"

"Door was unlocked," muttered Blaney.

"You *break into my house*, you accuse me of wild things, you yell and rant and rave about Glenda–" David threw his hands into the air in exasperation. "How on Earth do you even *know* Glenda?"

Blaney folded the aluminum foil back over the exposed casserole and cinched it in place. He nodded to himself as though coming to a decision. "From Minnie's Place," he said, looking up. "I first seen her at Minnie's Place."

David was unenlightened by this reply. "Who's Minnie?"

"You're kidding!" said Jeremy.

"What?" Once more, or still, or since forever, David was in the dark. "*Now* what?"

"You know," said Jeremy. "The place on Highway 104. Just across the county line. Crummy little cinderblock building."

David thought about it. Cinderblock... Now he remembered, or at least remembered the sign. On a metal pole by the highway. The pole and the sign both needed painting, as did the building. "Wait a minute," he said. "Are you talking about that *bar*? You're trying to say that Glenda was in a *bar*?"

"Friday night," said Blaney. He began again poking about the utensils on the table. "Friday night is her night."

This was simply too much. This wasn't *all* that was too much. Everything was too much. This was just more of too much. Too much more. But this, at least, would not stand.

"Well!" David shouted triumphantly. "Now I *know* you're lying!" He ran across the room and leaned on the table opposite Blaney. He shook a finger at him like a television prosecutor who has caught a witness in perjury. "That can't be true, Mr. Blaney! Glenda couldn't be in that place meeting you on Friday nights, because Glenda has a book club meeting at a girlfriend's house every Friday night! Some nights she even..." He stopped. Blaney picked up a fork, looked at it, then at David. They held one another's gaze across the casserole dish for several seconds, and the triumph on David's countenance drained away. "Sometimes," he murmured, "she even stays the night over there." He swallowed. "The last one they read was that book by that football player who found God after a head injury." His voice had become very small.

Blaney tapped the fork against the edge of the casserole dish. It gave off a tiny *ping* and a barely audible tone that faded quickly away. "I didn't know who she really was," Blaney said. "Not at first." He studied the fork in his hand. "She said her name was Trixie."

"*Trixie?*" David shrieked. There was a momentary screech of feedback from the intercom speaker.

"Whoa," said Jeremy.

"She..." Blaney turned away. Rolly Blaney at a loss for words was a strange sight. "I hadn't met nobody like her before. And me and her... We were..." He paused again, then wheeled around and angrily pointed the fork at David. "God damn it, Burkitt! If she was gonna leave you for anybody, it was supposed to be *me!*" He pivoted, aiming the fork at Jeremy. "And this little pissant? *Him?*"

Jeremy flinched. "I told you, man!" he protested, "If she's gone, it isn't with me! I haven't seen her since–"

"Since what!" Blaney's face was turning red. "Last Thursday? Thursday before *my* Friday?" He jammed the fork into the casserole hard enough to bend it.

There was a moment of relative quiet except for the continued low buzzing of the intercom speaker, raspier and not at all soothing like the control room's hum. Over it, David realized, he could hear his own heart beating. It sounded like a quick roll on a snare drum, the kind they play as the condemned man stands before the firing squad. His face felt warm. The room began to tilt. "Glenda?" he said, in the tone he used when he called out to her when she was in the next room. He did that sometimes. Called to her for no reason, just to hear her voice when she answered. "Glenda?" The TV studio faded. She was standing in front of him. She smiled at him, but her smile was different. "Glenda?" He felt that he was worn down, broken. He didn't have the strength, couldn't manage to continue to hold up the crushing weight of disbelief. He rolled the next words around, feeling them out like a phrase in an unknown language. "Glenda," he said at last, forcing it out, "has been unfaithful to me."

"Yes, I'm afraid so," said a voice. It wasn't Blaney, and it wasn't Jeremy. David blinked, tears fell onto his cheeks, and the room swirled into existence around him once more. He looked toward the voice. Deion Mullins, the TV station manager, stood in the hallway doorway. He stepped inside and closed the door behind him. "I'm afraid so, David," he repeated sadly. "And I hope that you can find it in your heart to forgive us."

David pitched forward, unconscious before his face hit the casserole.

<h1 style="text-align:center">14</h1>

When Margaret and Mrs. Sullivan fled the TV studio, they paused in the hallway to regroup. "Did you *ever*?" Mrs. Sullivan asked, to which Margaret replied, "No, child! I never did!" Mrs. Sullivan said, "We have to tell somebody. Who knows what they might do in there!" The reception desk was nearby, but no one was there. "This way," Mrs. Sullivan said, pointing up the hallway.

Deion Mullins was in his office, as was Laura, which explained the unmanned reception desk. They were in negotiations about some copying that Deion would have liked Laura to take care of for him, and the negotiations weren't going well for Deion. Laura usually preferred being called an "administrative assistant" rather than "receptionist," but her concept of her job title was ultimately fluid, often switching from "administrative assistant" back to "receptionist" when duties traditionally considered those of an administrative assistant were required of her. Deion typically foisted these kinds of negotiations off onto his wife, Mary, but she was over at the Great Rock helping to set up for the event that evening. Also, Laura was being even more sullen and difficult than usual today for some reason. Deion was on the point of his inevitable capitulation and decision to just go ahead and do the copying himself when Margaret and Mrs. Sullivan appeared in the doorway. Mrs. Sullivan waved a hand in the air at them as though flagging down a passing bus. "Mr. Mullins! Deion! Mr. Mullins!" Mrs. Sullivan never knew exactly how to address the station manager. He was the manager, after all. But on the other hand...

"Something wrong?" Deion asked.

"We believe you better come down to the studio. There's a situation in there."

"Situation?" Deion laid his stack of papers on the desk. Laura gave the two women a cold look, which Margaret returned whole-heartedly. Laura, Margaret felt, in addition to being stuck up, changed her hair color too frequently and dressed too young for herself.

"There's some kind of trouble in there! In the studio! Heaven help me, I believe they're having a fight!"

"What?" said Deion. "Who's having a fight?"

"I don't know for sure. Jeremy's in there, and another fella, and David Burkitt, I think. They're hollering and cussing and talking about Glenda!"

"Glenda?" Deion and Laura said the name simultaneously in similar tones of alarm.

"I thought this was a Christian TV station!" said Margaret. "But these fellas sound more like HBO! Not that I–"

Deion came around his desk and into the hallway. He started toward the studio, but stopped so abruptly that Margaret bumped into him. "You say David Burkitt is there? And they're talking about Glenda?"

"Hollering about her!" said Mrs. Sullivan.

"And using foul language," Margaret added.

Deion ran a hand across his mouth. The two women looked at one another. What was he waiting for? Why were they stalled in the hallway? Deion turned to them. "You two ladies stay here with Laura," he said.

"Do what?" Margaret objected.

"Ya'll stay here. I'll see to this. Just... Just stay!" He held out his hand out toward them like a dog trainer with inexperienced puppies. "Stay!" He backed away down the hall. The two women obeyed, though clearly as reluctant to do so as puppies would have been. Behind them Laura stepped out of the office. All three women watched Deion move down the hall and pause, his ear pressed against the studio door.

To their surprise, Deion grabbed the sides of the door frame with both hands and leaned against it, his head down as if suddenly weak, dizzy, or possibly in prayer. After a second he stood up straight again and took a step back. He drew himself up, raised his chin, and took a deep breath as if about to make a big entrance in a stage play. He stepped forward, opened the door and stood in the doorway. He said something that sounded like, "I'm afraid so," stepped into the studio and closed the door.

"Well what the Sam Hill was *that* about?" said Margaret.

"That," Laura said in a low, cold voice, "is what *I'd* like to know."

15

Vanity of vanities, saith the Preacher, vanity of vanities; all is vanity.

That's Ecclesiastes, thought David. Lots of Good Stuff in Ecclesiastes. No red print, but still.

The race is not to the swift, nor the battle to the strong. Time and chance happeneth to them all.

Better is a handful of quietness, than both the hands full with travail and vexation of spirit.

Good stuff.

Live joyfully with the wife whom thou lovest...

That which is crooked cannot be made straight...

He who increaseth knowledge increaseth sorrow.

David writhed in his bed. Why was everything so dark? It shouldn't be this pitch black, even in the middle of the night. The night light in the hallway...had the power gone off?

Voices. Loud voices. Somebody was arguing somewhere in the house. Who could it be? He didn't want to think about this. He just wanted to sleep. To sleep and sleep and sleep.

Glenda?

He stuck a hand out into the darkness, feeling for her. Why was the mattress so cold and hard?

If two lie together, then they have heat. But how can one be warm alone?

Somebody stepped on his hand.

David shouted in pain and sat up, not in his own bed, but on the floor of the studio at Channel 38. Everything remained dark, however. He put a hand to his face and was horrified. Something wet and sticky! He had a flash of gaping head wounds, oozing gray matter. He jerked his hand away and light shocked his eyes. He was holding some sort of silver mask. It was, in fact, the aluminum foil from the authentic taco casserole. It had molded itself to the shape of his visage and stuck there when his face plunged into the casserole dish.

Three people loomed above him: Jeremy, who had just stepped on his hand, Deion Mullins and Rolly Blaney. David's heart sank. The nightmare just wouldn't end, no matter how many times he woke up. Blaney had ahold of Deion's collar, and Jeremy seemed to be trying to intervene. Deion was shouting, "Let me loose! Turn me loose, I said!"

"Watch him, Deion!" Jeremy yelled, "Watch him, man! He'll choke you!"

"What the hell are you talking about?" Blaney twisted his fist, tightening his grip on Deion's shirt.

"I thought he knew!" Deion cried. "I thought that's what all the fuss was about!"

"You!" Blaney yelled, "You! Glenda and *you*?"

"Isn't that what the fuss was about?" Deion tried to pull away. "What was the fuss about?" Blaney pulled him back, and Jeremy stepped in. The three of them came staggering across the floor toward David.

"Stop! Stop! For the Love of God, *stop!*" David cried, and the three men froze and looked at him. "Stop...*stomping* me!" He tossed aside the aluminum mask and struggled to his feet, brushing damp lettuce and ground chuck from his necktie. His hair was a mess. His face was red. His shirttail was out. He began violently jamming it back into his pants.

Deion broke free from Blaney's grip. "I'm sorry, David," he said. "I'm sorry for what happened."

"Happened?" David moved to the table and leaned against it. There was the casserole, with a face-shaped dent in it. And there was that word again: Happened. It happened. It happened again. It just keeps on happening. *Why won't it stop happening?*

"Glenda is…" said Deion. He stopped, started over. "The temptation. It was just too strong! I love my wife! I do! But she's…"

"Fat?" said Blaney.

"Hey!" said Deion.

"Yeah," said Jeremy. "That's harsh."

"God damn!" Blaney cried, "One more and we can have a basketball team!" He put his hands on his hips and stalked around in a tight circle, stopped and pointed a finger at Deion. "You know what? I don't believe this shit for a minute. She wouldn't do that."

"Wouldn't do *what*?" Deion said. "What are trying to say?"

"You know what I'm saying."

Deion took a step toward Blaney. "Then why don't you just say it?"

"Hey guys!" Jeremy sounded frightened. "Come on, guys!"

David heard the exchange with little interest. He stood looking at the casserole. It didn't look half bad. He saw the bent fork stuck in one corner of the dish, pinning down a torn corner of aluminum foil. He pulled it out, dug out a glob of the casserole with it and put it in his mouth. Cold, but not half bad. No, not bad at all. He took another bite and tossed the fork aside. He was dimly aware of the voices getting louder. They bothered him. He decided to leave.

Too many surprises, too much noise, too much violence. His mind decided to give him a break. It checked out. His *brain* still worked. He could still walk, avoid obstacles, open doors. His *mind*, however, had left the premises. David was entering what the psychologists call a "dissociative state." He crossed the studio, passing directly between Deion and Blaney, who were faced off, hackles up, like two vicious dogs. He opened the door and walked into the hallway.

Three women sprang back from the door as he opened it. To the right were Margaret and Mrs. Sullivan, wide-eyed and amazed, surrounded by an almost visible cloud of curiosity. To the left was Laura, backing away toward the chair at the reception desk, her face blank, her eyes dead. David turned to his right. "Your casserole isn't half bad," he said.

"Oh!" said Mrs. Sullivan. "Uh… Thank you. The ground chuck costs a little more, but…" But David had turned away. He walked past the reception desk and paused to look at the poster on the wall.

KEEP

CALM

and

TRUST

JESUS

"Uh huh," he said. "Will do."

"Those men," said Laura.

David turned to look at her.

Something he was seeing pierced the fog of David's dissociative state. Laura had tears in her eyes. Laura? Tears? *Laura?* She pointed an orange fingernail at the studio door. "Those men," she said again. Then she let out what sounded for all the world like a sob, turned and ran, not easy given the tightness of her skirt, into the nearby ladies' room.

David stood and looked at the space Laura had just left. In a moment Margaret and Mrs. Sullivan moved into that space, mouths agape, looking at the ladies' room door. "Well what in the world…?" said Margaret.

The fog closed in again and David pivoted slowly away like a helium balloon in a very slight breeze. He gazed down the hallway toward the front doorway. Outside the glass doors stood Rolly Blaney's pickup truck.

16

David William Burkitt met Glenda Marie Roberts in Room 204 of the Buckalew Building, which all the students called the Buckaroo Building, on the campus of the same small state college whose growing Muslim enrollment would later so rile up Rolly Blaney. The Buckalew Building was given that strange appellation in honor of a long-dead man of the same name who once did something laudable, or possibly something deemed laudable at the time but now looked on with disapprobation or even horror, and who was connected to the origin of the college in some way that no one could clearly recall. Possibly his contribution was merely financial; the building with his name did house the Business Department.

David met Glenda in that room in that building because they were both in there attending an accounting class. It wasn't the first time David had seen Glenda or noticed her. He had seen her at what nowadays is called Baptist Campus Ministries but was then still called the Baptist Student Union, a religiously-affiliated campus organization that riled up no one at all. David had seen Glenda there, had most certainly noticed her, and had developed a deep affection for her. Her frequent attendance at the BSU was one of the things that attracted him, because David in college was already a deeply religious young man, and he admired Glenda's similar level of devotion. He had however, despite observing her quite often, never spoken to her. Had never even approached her. David had practically no experience approaching girls. Also, he considered Glenda Roberts, to his great sadness, pretty much out of his league.

What made Room 204 of the Buckalew Building different was that, while Glenda was a center of attention and a commanding presence at the BSU, in Accounting I she was somewhat at sea, while David was in his element. One day before class he overheard Glenda express to another student some mystification as to the precise difference between accruals and deferrals, and found himself boldly stepping in with a clarification. Glenda told him that if the textbook made things as clear as he did, she wouldn't have made a C-minus on the last test. He stammered his thanks and then, to his own utter astonishment, suggested that he would be happy to get together with her to go over some other accounting principles before the next test. To his further astonishment, she agreed.

Glenda got a B-plus on her next test, and their relationship began.

David saw flashes of this and other instants in their lives flitting before his mind's eye much as drowning men are said to see flashes of theirs. The analogy was an apt one since, much like a drowning man, David was gasping for breath, grasping vainly for support that wasn't there, and going in and out of consciousness. Unlike a drowning man, he was driving an ancient pick-up truck. He barely knew how to drive a stick shift of any kind, and this shifter on the steering column was a configuration he had never even seen before. The truck was also without power steering, which meant every turn found him straining and fighting the wheel like the helmsman of a trawler in a hurricane. The engine screamed constantly; exhaust fumes billowed around him; the vehicle bucked and jumped like an animal. It stalled at every stop sign and took several jerks and chokes to get going again. But even dealing with all of this could not stop the flashes of memory.

He and Glenda "went together" all through college. They met each other's parents. At the BSU he would play guitar while Glenda sang. Everyone agreed they were a perfect couple. Despite their feelings for one another, David suggested that they should "save themselves" for marriage. David then asked her to marry him. Immediately. She turned him down. She wasn't ready for marriage, she said. They should at least wait until after they graduated, she said. He said he understood, that he did not wish to pressure her. He would wait until they graduated. He was standing, ring in hand, at the foot of the steps when she came off the stage with her diploma.

She said she hadn't meant *right* after they graduated.

He said he would wait. He would wait forever, if it came to that, because to him there was no other woman in the world. Time passed. From time to time they discussed it. They prayed about it. They prayed about it some more. David prayed about it every day.

Finally, she said yes.

They were married by Reverend Horace Birdsong in the First Baptist Church, where they were active members. They moved into a small apartment. David worked for a bank. Glenda was a receptionist in a dentist's office. They saved their money. After five years, with a little assistance from David's parents, they bought a house. Over the last two years David started his own accounting business; Glenda became his part-time assistant and a Coca-Cola memorabilia entrepreneur. They became active in The Great Rock Church. They started their television show. Life was good. They were in love. They had no children, but they were still young. David hoped that one day...

One day.

The line of angry drivers queued up behind the bucking, smoking, grinding truck revved their engines and sped onward in great relief when he finally pulled off the road into a gravel parking lot. He hadn't realized where he was going, until he arrived. One last pop of the clutch and loud crash of the dying motor and there he was.

17

David paused to let his eyes adjust to the murkiness. In the meantime, he experienced the strange smells–there was the yeasty whang of what he assumed was spilled beer, some sort of industrial cleaner, a not-inconsequential layer of body odor. It was as if he were in a gym dressing room that had recently hosted a frat party. His vision gradually returned, starting with the lighted signs spelling out brands of beer and liquor, expanding to discern a low ceiling with dim light bulbs in recessed sockets; a scarred tile floor; tables, mostly empty, scattered about; booths, also mostly empty, lining one wall; a bar running along the wall opposite. One person, a man, sitting at the bar. He did not see, had not really thought he would see but somehow desperately in the very back of his mind hoped he might see, a familiar face.

So this was Minnie's Place.

At one end of the room was a low riser with a drum set pushed back against the wall, a ragged hole in the bass drum. Fronting the riser was a scuffed wooden dance floor, barely larger than David's front porch. Next to the riser, as either backup or, as seemed more likely given the state of the bandstand, primary music source for the establishment, stood a jukebox. It was currently playing a country song. To David's relief it was an "I'm proud to be an American" country song, not a "cheating" country song.

A woman carrying a tray with bottles on it passed by. She was in her twenties, wore cut-off jeans and a tank top, and had a lot of brown hair tied into a loose knot atop her head. "Come on in, honey!" she said, and moved on.

David walked toward the bar.

The man seated at the bar was a wiry fellow with short, sandy hair. He had one weathered boot on the brass rail and the other on a strut of his barstool. He wore a gray shirt which had, David saw as he walked up and stood next to him, a red-and-white name patch on the right breast. *Larry.* The man glanced up at David, revealing a pointy nose and sleepy, deep-set eyes.

The bartender approached. He was a large man, middle-aged, with thinning hair pulled into a ponytail and a mustache that hooked up with a pair of muttonchop sideburns like a Civil War general. The ponytail, along with a leather or possibly fake leather vest over a t-shirt, gave him a vaguely "biker" air. His expression seemed to David wary, almost hostile. "You A.B.C.?" he said.

Am I what? David looked at "Larry," who was also studying him suspiciously. Taking what seemed to be the safe route he replied, "No. No, I'm not."

The bartender still seemed unsure, but said, "What can I get you?"

What indeed? What could he be gotten? He had not planned to get anything. He hadn't planned anything at all, least of all coming here. Now that he had arrived, despite having only the lowest of expectations, he was still underwhelmed. It wasn't even a bar, really. Not a legitimate bar like the ones you waited in, sipping your iced tea, while they got your table ready in a restaurant. This was a joint. A *beer joint.* But Glenda, it seemed, had visited it. Regularly. Glenda. *His* Glenda, in a *beer joint.* But was that right? Here, she wasn't even Glenda! David reached out and laid a hand on the rough wood of the bar. Had *Trixie* sat right here, perhaps?

Was Rolly Blaney sitting next to her?

David snatched his hand away as though burned.

By now the muttonchop man was even more suspicious. "Hey," he said, with a *what's up with him?* glance at Larry, "You hear me?

What can I get you?" David looked at him. This man had walked up to *her* and asked the same question. How had she answered?

I need some things that you can't give me…

David shifted his gaze to the vast array of bottles on the wall behind the man. So many different varieties of what, after all, was pretty much the same thing, wasn't it? "Be not drunk with wine," he murmured, "but filled with the spirit."

"How's that?" said the bartender, cocking his head.

"Ephesians," said David. "But, on the other hand, 'Eat thy bread and drink thy wine with a merry heart!'" He smiled at their slack faces. "Ecclesiastes. Lots of good stuff in Ecclesiastes." He pointed at the brown bottle on the bar in front of the man next to him. "What are you having?"

The man sat up, not sure he wanted to be dragged into this. He looked at the bottle. "Bud," he said cautiously.

"Is that any good?"

He seemed to consider, as though the question had never occurred to him before. He shrugged. "It's awright."

But David had now had a thought. "No," he said. "Whiskey." He gave a sharp nod. "I will have a glass of whiskey. And *Coke*. Whiskey. And Coke." That's what *she* would have had. He somehow knew it. He tapped the bar before him with a fingertip. The bartender and Larry looked at each other. They hadn't heard a drink order given with such an air of profundity before.

"Whiskey and Coke?" the bartender repeated.

"Yes." Another confident nod, then: "That's a thing, right?"

"Yeah, that's a thing."

"All right." David nodded again, at Larry this time. "Then that's what I'll have."

"Jack alright?" asked the bartender.

David waved a hand. "I don't care who makes it. Just… Whiskey and Coke."

"Uh huh." The two men exchanged another look. "You want to start a tab?"

"You bet! Why not?"

"Credit card?"

"Hmm? Oh!" David took out his wallet and handed a Discover card to the bartender. The bartender looked at it dubiously, slung his towel across his shoulder and walked away. David leaned on the bar. There. He had ordered a drink. And when it came, he would drink it. He noticed that "Larry" was still studying him. "Not a big drinker, huh?" said the man.

"I had a frozen margarita once in a Mexican restaurant," said David. "It gave me a headache."

"Well, that's most likely just your brain freeze," said Larry, leaning an elbow on the bar. "Bet you anything that's what that was."

"Oh?"

"Anything real cold will do it, you drink it too fast."

"Yes, now that you mention it, you may be right. Brain freeze. Yes."

Larry's eyes narrowed. "Do I know you from somewhere? You look familiar."

"I don't think so." David watched the bartender. He had poured something into a glass from a bottle and was adding something else from a hose under the bar. "What's A.B.C. mean?"

"Alcoholic Beverage Control," said Larry. "They send people around sometimes to check on places. Make sure they're following the booze rules. Ain't selling to minors, that kinda thing. And you do look a little narky. No offense."

David considered his khaki trousers and buttoned-down shirt and looked around the room. Though badly stained with sour cream, his was definitely the only necktie in evidence.

The bartender approached and set a glass and David's credit card on the bar. David pocketed the card and picked up the glass. He studied it. It didn't look that different from a regular glass of cola, except it seemed to glow a lighter brown around the ice cubes. He saw that Larry and the bartender were watching him. Larry lifted his beer bottle in a small "here's to you" gesture. David took a drink.

In movies the greenhorn who takes his first drink of whiskey always chokes and coughs and spews, at which point the grizzled cowhands burst into laughter. David was fully prepared for this scenario, minus the grizzled cowhands, but to his surprise the drink wasn't that bad. There was a sort of chemical "whang" to it, and a slight burning as it went down, but mainly it just seemed sweet. He smacked his lips. "Not bad," he said. The bartender and Larry relaxed, neither sure why he had been tense in the first place.

David took another sip and looked at Larry. "You want one?"

"Huh?" Larry grunted.

"One of these for my friend here," David said. "On me." That was something else that happened in movies.

Larry sat up and grinned. "Thanks, buddy!"

"Don't mention it." David looked around the room. "Can I take this over there?"

"Sure," said the bartender.

David, careful not to spill any of his drink, made his way to a table near the jukebox. The song playing when he entered had ended, and the jukebox, after a clunk like two train cars coupling, started another. Fiddle. Steel guitar. A woman this time. She loved her man. Naturally. With country music you can't avoid the irony for long. He took a deep swallow of the liquid. He watched the waitress approach. She seemed in his opinion much too young to work in a place like this. "Did you want a menu, hon?"

"Menu?" David said. "You serve food here?"

"Well," she waggled a hand. "Sorta. Chips and dip. Cheese sticks. You know. Bar food."

David realized he'd had nothing but two forkfuls of faux taco casserole since breakfast, and breakfast had only been a convenience store honey bun. But he didn't feel hungry. He didn't feel much of anything. "Not right now," he said, and took another sip of his drink.

"OK," said the girl, "Let me know if you change your mind. I'm Cindy."

"Thank you, Cindy." She started away, but David raised a hand. "Oh! Just a second!" He hesitated. "Has, uh..." He was on the edge of asking, *has Trixie been in lately*? but found he couldn't do it. "Uh... As long as you're here..." He tipped back the drink and chugged down the rest, held out the empty glass. "Bring me another one of these, would you please?"

Cindy took the glass. "Well, OK then," she said with a chuckle. "What is it?"

"Uh..."

"Jack and Coke," said a voice. "Make it two, beautiful." It was Larry. He had approached behind Cindy, his own drink in hand. He stepped up to the table. Cindy looked at David, and when he didn't object to Larry's addition to the order, moved toward the bar. "Mind?" Larry asked, but he was already pulling out a chair and dropping into it.

David pointed across the room to the bar. "I thought Jack was the bartender."

Larry laughed. "You're a stitch, buddy! Thanks again for the drinks." He raised his glass.

Drinks, plural. On David's tab. That was... David tried to think of the word "presumptuous," but it wouldn't come. His head felt a little light. Surely the drink didn't work that fast?

"Man," said Larry, "I can't get over the feeling I know you from somewhere. You ever get your car worked on at Collins Texaco?"

"No," said David. For maintenance he always dealt strictly with the dealership. A little more expensive perhaps, but you could be sure of the proper parts and so on. He refrained from explaining this to Larry.

Larry shook his head. "Weird. Maybe you just look like somebody."

David was not in the mood for conversation, but even now his innate politeness would not let him come right out and say so. "Or maybe somebody looks like me."

Larry laughed again, too loudly. "I like you, buddy," he said. He stuck out a hand. "Larry Corley."

"David Burkitt." David extended his own hand, and Larry grabbed and shook it vigorously.

"Burkitt," Larry mused. David pulled his hand free. "Damn, that sounds familiar, too! It's gonna drive me crazy 'til I can figure it out."

"Crazy," David repeated. There was definitely something going on in his head. He couldn't be sure if it was related to the alcohol or if he was simply losing his mind. Both seemed equally likely. He looked at the hand Larry had just shaken. His fingers were tingling. "That Jack whiskey," he said, "That's pretty strong stuff?"

"Oh, middling," Larry said. "Middling stout. Ain't the stoutest. There's some way stouter. Jack's pretty pricey, too."

"Oh?" David realized he hadn't even asked what a drink cost.

"Oh yeah. Kentucky Tavern for instance? That's bourbon whiskey, too." Larry held up his glass. "For what you've laid out for these, you coulda got a fifth."

"A fifth of what?"

"Of Kentucky Tavern!"

This guy must be drunk, David thought. *He isn't making any sense.* "What's the other eighty percent?"

Larry looked confused. "Well, anyway," he said, "my point is there's cheaper ways to get there from here. If you catch my meaning. Matter of fact," he snapped his fingers, "you know what? That gives me an–"

"Here you are!" Cindy was back with two more glasses. She set them on the table.

"How's that for quick service!" Larry said, sliding his new drink over next to the old one. "You're a angel of mercy, darling. Pretty as a angel, too, ain't she?" Cindy smiled a tight smile at David, but the smile disappeared when she looked at Larry. She walked away. Larry watched her go and gave a sharp intake of breath. "Godamighty," he said. "Ain't that ass something?" He dropped his voice conspiratorially. "I been working on that. For quite a while." He gave a lascivious wink. "And I'm getting close. *Real* close." David picked up his glass and took a deep swallow. He was regretting his earlier magnanimity.

Larry took a swig from his first drink and pulled the new one close to him protectively. "Anyway, what I was fixing to say was, you want to save some money, why not buy a bottle of something? Even Jack Daniels, that's a lot cheaper by the bottle than by the glass."

Jack had a last name? "A whole bottle?" David said. What had happened to buying one fifth of something? Can you have a fifth of a bottle? Wouldn't that just be a smaller bottle?

"Yeah. Way better deal," Larry went on. "At the liquor store."

"What?" David wasn't following any of this now. "What liquor store? We're in a bar."

"Yeah, right. But if we go to the liquor store, you can pick us up a bottle! Hell yeah! That's what we'll do! This place is dead anyway. What do you say we go to the store, you get us a bottle of Jack, and then you and me can–"

"I'll tell you what you can do. You can get your ass out of my chair."

The voice seemed to come from nowhere. David twitched, and some of the precious, apparently expensive "Jack" hopped into the air. He raised his eyes from the glass to find Rolly Blaney standing at the table, and to multiply his surprise and deepen his dismay, behind him, looking extremely dismayed himself, stood Jeremy.

18

"The hell do *you* want, Blaney?" said Larry, his friendly, wheedling tone gone.

"You heard me. Get out of my chair."

"*Your* chair?" Larry gestured toward David. "Me and this fella are having a conversation. Who the hell are you to–"

"Five seconds, asshole," said Blaney, "then I'm kicking your ass out into the parking lot."

Larry defiantly stood, or rather sat, his ground for three of the five seconds, then the chair scraped back from the table. He grabbed up both of his glasses and stood. "One of these days, Blaney," he snarled, and moved away toward another table.

"Go fuck yourself, Corley," said Blaney. He yanked the chair around and sat. "Nobody else will." His back now to Larry, Blaney acted as if he had never existed. He pointed to another chair across the table and said to Jeremy, "Have a seat." Jeremy sat.

David watched Larry slink away. "I take it," he said, "you two have met."

Blaney fixed David with a hostile stare. "Hell of a thing to take a man's truck," he said.

"*What?*" David's voice rose in both pitch and volume. "Take a man's *truck?* Oh, yes! So sorry! A terrible thing! A terrible thing to violate another man's sacred, holy bond with his *truck!*" Jeremy looked around nervously. If Blaney was bothered by the outburst, he didn't show it. David gulped his drink and returned Blaney's stare.

"I had to ask Godspell here–" Blaney jerked a thumb at Jeremy, "--to give me a ride."

"*Ask* me?" yelped Jeremy. "Technically, I think I've been kid-napped!"

"*Technically*," said Blaney, "you've been abducted. Kidnapping requires a demand for ransom. Now shut up." To David: "When you wasn't home, I took a wild guess that you might come here. You didn't tear my truck up, did you?"

"How would you even tell?" said David. He took another drink.

Blaney pointed at David's glass. "What is that?"

"None of your business." He took another swig.

"That truck is a classic, you know. And the transmission is touchy."

"Well, don't worry. I only used one gear. Where's Deion? Didn't he want to join the party?"

"Nevermind about him."

"Holy moly," said Jeremy. "You should have seen how–"

"Didn't I tell you to shut up?" Blaney said.

David finished off the drink. Cindy was passing nearby, and he waved at her. "Cindy! Yoohoo!"

"'Yoohoo?'" said Blaney. "How many of them have you had?"

"None of your business," David repeated.

Cindy arrived at the table. She gave Blaney's shoulder a quick squeeze. "Hello, Rolly!"

"Hi, Cin."

"What do ya'll need?"

"Another of these, please, Cynthia," said David.

Cindy giggled. "Is this a friend of yours, Rolly?"

"Acquaintance," said Blaney.

She turned to Jeremy. "Get you something, hon?"

"Uh..." Jeremy leaned over to look toward the bar as though ex-pecting to see a menu on the wall. "What kind of coffee do you–"

"Bring him a Coke," said Blaney.

"I don't want–" Blaney looked at him. Jeremy slumped in his chair. "Bring me a Coke."

"And you, hon? The usual?"

"Yeah," said Blaney.

Cindy turned to go, but David called her back. "Wait a minute! Wait! Usual? What is that? What's his usual?"

"Jameson. Rocks."

"Rocks means ice, right?" He looked at Jeremy. "Why don't they just say 'ice?'" Jeremy shrugged. "Jameson. Is that like Jack?"

"Well, it's a different kind of–"

"I'll have that." David thumped the table with a fist. "Mr. Rolly Blaney's 'usual' is the magic elixir, right? So I'll have that. What he's having. And double it. A double of it. However you say it."

"OK then." Cindy looked doubtful but headed for the bar.

"I thought you didn't drink, Burkitt," said Blaney.

"You don't know what I don't do. I do a lot of things I don't do. Why are you here, anyway?" Of all the uncharitable feelings David had ever had, and right now there were a lot of uncharitable feelings spread over a surprising–not to say shocking–number of people, the least charitable feelings of all were his feelings for Rolly Blaney. "Your truck's outside. Take it and go."

"I'm here because we ain't done."

"Your grammar is terrible, you know that? And what do you mean? We *am* done. I am. Done." He made a chopping motion with a hand, miscalculated the distance and banged the edge of the table. With great difficulty he managed not to wince.

"Man," said Jeremy. "For myself, you know... I just want to say... Hey, you know?" He shook his head, looked genuinely distressed. "I'm just... I want you to know... I mean... I'm just..." David stared at him, wondering if this would ever resolve into anything. "I'm just...really sorry. About... About...you know...everything."

David gave a sudden anguished yell. It simply burst out, surprising him as much as everyone else within earshot, which was everyone in the place. Jeremy recoiled. Heads turned toward them all over the room. It was that word. *Everything.* That *everything* involved things that David could never have imagined, even if he had been asked to imagine *everything*.

The bartender called out, "Ya'll all right over there?" Blaney raised a hand and waved it dismissively. David rubbed his eyes and sighed. "Excuse me," he said, partly to Jeremy and partly to the room in general. He abruptly leaned toward Jeremy. "Why an afghan?" he asked. "Why not a blanket?" Jeremy stared at his hands, clasped before him on the table.

"Listen, Burkitt," Blaney said impatiently. "Here's the way I see it. You got grievances. Fair enough. But there's other issues going on here. And you ain't the only one."

"What issues? And what do you mean I ain't the– I'm not the only one? The only one what?"

"With grievances."

David wasn't sure he was hearing this correctly. Maybe it was the garbled grammar. "Are you telling me now that you think *you* have grievances?"

"You're damn right."

Within his chest, along with a burning sensation, David felt the unfamiliar swell of rising indignation. "Why would *you* have a grievance?"

"You ain't the only one who got blindsided."

"You know what I think?" David pointed a shaky finger at Blaney. "I think you're *jealous*. Because I got a note, and you didn't. Because *Glenda* left her husband a note, but *Trixie!*" He was unable to say the name without shrieking it in disbelief. "--Didn't leave one for...whatever you are!" He rounded on Jeremy again. "How about you? Do *you* have 'grievances?'" Jeremy couldn't meet David's gaze, and David's gaze dropped from Jeremy's face to the young man's chest. "Wait a minute," he said. "What is that?"

"Huh?" Jeremy looked down at his t-shirt. It was blue and featured three golden crosses, one tall in the center, with the two outer ones curved to create a double-arched "M" shape. Underneath were the words, *Over a Billion Saved.*

"That's not the..." David began. He looked at Blaney. "He was wearing a shirt with a Star Trek thing on it. Before. You saw it. And before that there was one with a mustache."

Jeremy plucked at his shirt front. "It's just a shirt," he said.

"Yes, but when did you have time to change it?" He swiveled toward Blaney. "Did you see him change it?"

"God dammit, Burkitt," Blaney growled.

"I just want to know how– Oh! Here we go!" Cindy was approaching with a tray holding three glasses. She set a tall, dark one in front of Jeremy and shorter, half-filled glasses in front of Blaney and David. "And this is... What is this again?"

"Jameson," said Cindy. She shot another worried look at Blaney. "Straight, on the rocks. It's what you wanted, right?"

David picked up his glass and studied it. This new stuff was a lighter color than his earlier drinks. Did that mean it was weaker? "So how is this different from the 'Jack'?" he asked. He was developing a great interest in the distiller's art.

"Well," said Cindy, "Jack Daniels is bourbon whiskey. Made in Tennessee. And that–"

David tipped the glass up, took a moderately deep swallow, and went into convulsions. Here was the "movie greenhorn takes his first drink" response which he had anticipated earlier, but which had failed to take place. This new liquid burned; it robbed him of breath. He coughed and choked. His eyes filled with tears.

"And that's Irish," said Blaney.

David set the glass down on the table and pushed it away. He gasped for breath. He managed to choke out the word, "Water!" Cindy turned and ran for the bar.

Blaney drummed his fingers on the table. "All right, Burkitt," he said, "You done with the floor show?"

David coughed out, "Why won't you just–"

Blaney slammed a fist down on the table. "Do you want to find her or not?"

David gave one more cough, followed by a deep breath. He and Blaney looked at each other for a long moment. David swallowed. "Yes," he said.

"All right then. The first thing we need to do–"

"I know who you are now!"

David looked up to find Larry standing behind Blaney's chair wearing a broad grin. They had ceased to notice him, but he had only retreated as far as the next table, where he sat nursing his drinks and his grudge while eavesdropping on their conversation. When he heard David say the name *Glenda*, then yelp the name *Trixie*, his face had broken into an evil grin. Now he pointed a finger at David and walked around to stand across from him. "Burkitt! I knew I knew that name. You're that squeaky little bastard on that TV show! On the Jesus Channel. My mama keeps that channel on day and night. I seen you on there a bunch of times. You and your wife!"

David was recognized from time to time in grocery stores or restaurants, but he certainly had not anticipated being recognized here. Blaney said, "Piss off, Corley."

"Naw, naw!" Larry said, waving Blaney away with a laugh. "Holy shit! I see it now! I get it! On karry-okey night, you know, when she would get up and sing. I *knew* I'd heard her somewhere. I thought she just sounded like somebody on the radio, but it wasn't the radio. It was the TV!"

"Corley!" Blaney's voice was a low growl, and he put both hands on the table as though about to lever himself to his feet. Larry paid no attention, caught up as he was in the hilarity.

"It was her!" Larry looked around the room and raised his voice. "Trixie! Ya'll know Trixie! Trixie is the Jesus TV woman! Holy shit! I didn't recognize her with the blond wig, but it was her!"

Blond wig? David tried to say something, but couldn't.

"You know! Trixie!" Larry addressed the curious faces turned their way. "The one who danced on the bar on St. Patrick's Day!" He raised a hand high to point David out. "That was his wife!"

How? David thought. *How can things as bad as they can possibly be keep getting worse and worse and worse?*

Larry now turned to Blaney. "And you!" He was howling with laughter now. "Ol' Rolly Blaney's been sticking it to the–"

Blaney came in low like a pro lineman, slammed a shoulder into Larry's stomach, lifted him off his feet and slammed him down onto a neighboring table. The table's occupants fell out of their chairs, and the table tipped over, dumping the two men onto the floor, where they landed punching and cursing. A woman screamed. The roaring voice of the bartender shouted, "Hey! Take it outside!" This had no effect on the two men, who rolled across the room knocking patrons over like bowling pins.

"Holy smokes!" Jeremy yelled. "They're gonna kill each other!"

"Hm," said David, nodding absently. He was digging into his wallet for a five-dollar bill to leave on the table for Cindy. He put the wallet back in his hip pocket. "Can you give me a ride, please?" he asked.

"A ride?" Jeremy said distractedly. "Where?" Blaney had gotten to his feet. He aimed a kick at Corley's head, but Corley managed to grab his leg and Blaney went down again. Both went rolling across the floor once more.

"The liquor store." David picked up the glass in front of him and tossed the rest of its contents down his throat. Then he picked up Blaney's untouched glass and stumbled off with it, coughing, through the roiling and shouting crowd toward the door.

19

The term "fifth," it turned out, sometimes refers to a particular standard size of liquor bottle. David managed to determine this after a certain amount of Abbott and Costello back-and-forth with the proprietor of County Line Liquor, though he still wasn't clear what the larger amount was that the fifth was one-fifth of. "Who the hell knows?" the man behind the counter snapped, patience gone at last. "Do you want the bottle or not?"

David did. He finished the drink in his hand, set the empty glass on the counter along with some money, picked up the bottle and walked out to the car where Jeremy waited, chewing his fingernails.

Jeremy had tried to talk David into going straight home and out of the stop at the liquor store, which was located thirty feet before they crossed back into their own dry county. David, however, was adamant, and Jeremy's guilt combined with David's frankly unnerving new demeanor made him give it up and follow instructions. Adding to his distress, on their way down Highway 104 back toward the county line they met a police car, siren blaring, heading the other way. That seemed to indicate that the fracas at Minnie's Place had continued to escalate.

David climbed awkwardly into the passenger seat with his bottle cradled in his arms and pointed. "Home, Jerms," he said.

On the way from the liquor store to David's house, Jeremy felt compelled to attempt once more, with similar eloquence unfortunately, to express his deep regret and earnest self-reproach for what had happened between himself and Glenda. When he got to her name, he stammered himself into several seconds of complete incomprehensibility, since using her first name seemed awkward due to the implication–reminder, rather–of intimacy, but the alternative (Mrs. Burkitt) was, given the circumstances, even worse. Plowing inartfully on, he then began, as people who feel guilty often will, to veer slightly away from pure contrition toward just a tiny bit of self-justification. He wanted to assure David that there had been no improper or untoward approaches on his own part. On the contrary, the whole...*thing* began as a result of some very aggressive moves on Glenda's. Shockingly aggressive, in fact. So shocking, in fact, that the first time it happened–

At this point David let out another loud, wordless cry. Jeremy almost ran off the road. After that, he kept quiet.

David, once he had compelled Jeremy to for the love of God shut up, tried to think. He was remembering what Blaney had said. *Do you want to find her or not?* Yes. Yes, he did. He did want to find her. That was why he had gone to that awful Minnie place, not even knowing at the time that that was where he was going. In spite of all the revelations crashing down on him like meteorites, in spite of all the evidence that there was another Glenda–multiple Glendas– whom he had never known and whose existence he had never even imagined, somewhere among them had to be *his* Glenda, and he had to find her. He had to know why this had to happen. Their life could not have been *all* a charade, not for all those years. Could it? And why now? Why did it all end now, suddenly and abruptly? Also, although the suggestion had at first enraged him, he had to admit that Blaney had at least a small shred of a point: She hadn't abandoned only him. All the Glendas had disappeared at once.

The first thing we need to do is... Blaney had begun that sentence just before that horrible man popped up in front of them. What was he about to say? David had no idea about the first thing to do, not even the slightest, lightest shadow of an idea. And so, with a burning desire to do something and no clue whatsoever as to what that something might be, and with his energy waning along with the strange, almost euphoric feeling he had briefly experienced in the bar, he now just wanted to make it all go away. All of it. His grip tightened on the bottle in his lap.

"Looks like there's somebody on your porch," said Jeremy.

They had reached David's house. It was getting dark, and as the car turned into the driveway the headlights swept across the house and yard. There was a strange car behind his own in the driveway, and a figure turned from the door on which he had been in the process of knocking, shading his eyes against the harsh light.

"Hey," said Jeremy. "It's Deion."

"Oh good," said David. "That's fine. That's just fine." David opened the door and began to step out of the car while it was still rolling. Jeremy abruptly brought it to a stop. "Thanks for the ride."

David walked across the yard toward his door, head down. Deion stepped back as he approached. "David," he said, "I'm glad you got here. We need to talk."

"Oh," David said, clutching the bottle to his chest and digging in his pocket for his keys, "I don't think that's necessary."

"But it is," Deion intoned. "David. I've wronged you. I've wronged my wife."

"OK," said David. He switched hands on the bottle and dug frantically in his other pocket.

"I've wronged myself," Deion went on, "and I've wronged my God!"

"My God," David echoed, and then he remembered that his door was not locked. He grabbed the doorknob and stepped inside. He turned back with the intention of slamming the door after saying something along the lines of, "Point taken," or possibly just, "Got it!" To his horror, however, Deion was striding into the room past him. "I couldn't just let it go," he said.

"You could, though," said David. "You really–"

"I have to try to make it right. Who's that?" To David's continued horror, Jeremy appeared in the doorway and also stepped into his house. "Hey, Deion," he said.

"Jeremy?" Deion said, "What are you doing here?"

"I gave Dave a ride home. I just wanted to step in to tell you sorry."

"Tell *me* sorry?"

"That I'm not at the station. Figured you'd be worried."

"Why would I be worried?"

"The show tonight from the church?" Jeremy prompted. "The big special?"

"Janie is there on the switcher. Look, Jeremy, David and I—"

"Well, yeah, but with the special show and everything, I figured you'd want me there, too."

"All it takes," said Deion, "is to punch the button that says Church Feed."

"Well, yeah," said Jeremy, "but you know… Janie's just, you know, Janie. And this is a special show and everything. Thought you'd want the Engineer on hand."

"Janie's quite capable of–"

David sadly realized that holding the door meaningfully open was having no effect other than letting in mosquitos. He sighed, closed it, and walked into the kitchen, pausing to turn on the light. He pulled his phone from his pocket and checked it. The battery was almost dead, and there were no calls or texts. Should he try again? He dropped the phone onto the table with a clunk. If she hadn't answered the first eighteen or twenty, she wasn't going to start now.

Bitsy the cat sat in the middle of the kitchen floor, looking at him accusingly. "Morrow," she said petulantly. "Ow."

"All right," David said. He set the bottle carefully on the counter and opened the cabinet that held the container of cat food.

"Hey, Dave," said Jeremy from the living room, "do you mind if we turn on your TV? To check the station?"

"There's nothing wrong at the station!" said Deion.

"It's David," said David. "No one calls me..." A blue light flared up in the dark living room. A man's amplified voice began to speak. David moved to Bitsy's dish in the corner, poured food into it and also onto Bitsy's head, since she leapt in to start eating as soon as the first kibbles hit the bowl. David watched the cat. Bitsy, he realized, had been abandoned, too. He felt a sudden pang of pity for both himself and the animal. He reached down to pet her, which occasioned a sharp hiss and baring of fangs. He snatched his hand back.

The hand that feeds you.

He turned and reached for the bottle.

The raspy voice from the television in the other room said, "And I will remove thy candlestick out of his place, except thou repent!" He recognized the strident tones of TV evangelist Hiram Gobel. "'Thou hatest the deeds of the Nicolaitans, which I also hate.' What's this candlestick business, you ask? Well, I don't know. But let's us just talk about them Nicolaitans, shall we?"

This one was a rerun, David realized. The hated Nicolaitans, if he recalled correctly, were some sort of early form of Democrat, apparently. In this episode of his show, Hiram, as usual, was reading from the Book of Revelation, Hiram's personal favorite. Not much Good Stuff, David thought with a sad chuckle, in Revelation.

Behold, I will cast her into a bed, and them that commit adultery with her into great tribulation...

David spasmed. Things were thinking themselves in his head now without his input or authorization. Since he had gripped the bottle's cap, his spasm had the effect of twisting it. The plastic seal crackled loudly. He sniffed the bottle's cap and recoiled. It seemed to burn his nose hairs. Clearly, the trick was to dilute the stuff. He'd learned that much, at least.

Hiram harangued on. Jeremy was saying that the color seemed off, something about a vectorscope, and should he call Janie? Deion's reply sounded grumpy. David got a glass from the cabinet, went to the refrigerator, and got out a two-liter bottle of cola. He wasn't sure about what the proportions of the two liquids should be. Maybe the mysterious "fifth" came into play here? He began to try to estimate one fifth of the glass. That was assuming, of course, that the proportions weren't the other way around. But wait. The glass was not a perfect cylinder. It flared toward the top. It wasn't as simple as just filling it one fifth of the way up. Working out one fifth of the volume of a non-uniform container would require calculus or something, wouldn't it? He had taken calculus in college. Maybe it would come back to him. Somewhere he had a graphing calculator...

A buzzing noise had arisen in his head. He shook it sharply. *What's wrong with me?*

He splashed the glass roughly half full of whiskey and dumped in a splash of cola, pausing to let the fizz recede. In the living room, Hiram Goble was now going off on the Whore of Babylon. Beast with seven heads. Drunk on the blood of saints. David shuddered. *Lots of Scary Stuff in Revelation.* That was probably why Brother Birdsong almost never referenced it in his sermons. The thought of Brother Birdsong made David frown. Remembering Brother Birdsong's strange behavior that day brought another memory bobbing to the surface of his roiling mind.

He took a drink from his glass, coughed for several seconds, and burped.

20

The memory was from some earlier–decades? No, not that long. In his current state time wasn't very fixed in his mind. He and Glenda were sitting side by side in their pew at First Baptist Church. "Their" pew was third row back, left side, middle. They were so regular in this that David left things—Sunday school fliers, his notebook (he sometimes took notes), his Sunday Bible—in the little hymnal holder on the back of the pew in front of them. Scattered in the pews around them the other parishioners shifted and fidgeted, sniffed and occasionally coughed. Glenda sat on his right, his right hand clasping her left, as it did every Sunday. His left hand held his Bible.

The sermon for that morning, according to the program, was to be something from the Book of Isaiah. But Brother Birdsong had changed his mind at the last minute, telling the congregation instead to turn to the fourth chapter of the Gospel of John. David dutifully did so and laid the open Bible on his leg.

"I want to talk today about Jesus's meeting," Brother Birdsong began, "with the Samaritan woman at Jacob's Well. We don't know the woman's name. She's generally just called, kind of obviously, the Woman at the Well."

David knew the story. It wasn't one of the biggies, but it was among those New Testament stories that most people knew if they knew any at all. Brother Birdsong ran down the main points: Very early in his ministry, Jesus stops to rest at a well in Samaria while his disciples go into town to buy food. A Samaritan woman comes up to draw water, and Jesus asks her to give him a drink. The woman is surprised, since Jews didn't usually even talk to Samaritans, much less drink after them. Jesus tells her that if she knew who she was talking to, she'd ask *him* for a drink, because he offered Living Water.

"You can imagine what the woman must have thought," said Brother Birdsong. "Living Water? What the heck is this crazy Jew talking about?" The congregation tittered nervously. There were a few disapproving coughs. Not everyone felt it was acceptable to refer to Jesus as "crazy," even in jest. A few members weren't completely comfortable being reminded that He was a Jew.

"Jesus, of course," Brother Birdsong went on, "was talking about his Message. He says whoever drinks this well water will be thirsty again in no time, but drink the water of God's Word and you'll have everlasting life." He paused, shook his head. "Sometimes you have to wonder why Jesus didn't just say what he meant." No titters this time. He went on. "So the woman says, OK, let me try some of this 'living water.' And Jesus says..." Again he paused, looking down at his Bible on the pulpit before him. David realized that Brother Birdsong, usually one for continuous eye contact, which was one way to keep listeners on their toes and paying attention, had not been looking their way at all today.

"Jesus tells her," Brother Birdsong started again, "go and get your husband." Now he looked up. David smiled as Brother Birdsong looked their way–he always liked to show encouragement–but the preacher only gave them a brief glance before turning away.

"This is where Jesus is being kind of crafty. He's playing, well, you might almost say a mean trick on her. The woman says, "Oh! I... Uh... Ahem! I don't *have* a husband." But Jesus already knows that!" Brother Birdsong gave a sly look and shook an index finger in the air. "He's Jesus, after all! But that isn't all he knows. Now Jesus says, "But you've had *five* 'husbands,' haven't you? And you're with a man now, and he isn't your husband at all." Brother Birdsong gave an exaggerated wink on each of the "husbands." No titters anywhere this time, and the coughing and fidgeting had also stopped. David felt Glenda pull her hand away.

Brother Birdsong paused again, seeming to collect himself. "The woman," he went on, more quickly, "is amazed. How does this stranger know all about her? She realizes that he must be a prophet, a Holy Man. Well, in fact, as we know, He is *the* Holy Man. He is the Messiah. The woman drops her water jug and runs back into town and starts telling everybody about it. And when Jesus comes into town, the people are primed and ready to listen, and they do. Many of them accept him as Christ, the Savior of the world. So this woman, this *sinful* woman, had become what some might think of as Jesus' first evangelist." He chuckled. "Sorry, boys!" Again, no titters. He became more serious. "That's the story. Now, here's my point."

David looked at Glenda. A change had come over her—a stiffening of her posture, a different tilt of her head. He leaned slightly forward to try to catch her eye, but she didn't turn his way.

"Let's consider the nature of this 'woman at the well,'" said Brother Birdsong. "She was a Samaritan, yes, and the folks of Judea didn't like Samaritans. We know that much. Samaritans had such a bad reputation that there was only ever one 'Good' one, and he became a celebrity because of it." A few titters once more. They all liked an inside joke. "But what I mean is her *moral character*. This stuff about five so-called husbands and how she isn't married to the one she's with now. Why would Jesus pick a woman like that to carry His message to the town? Why not go to the mayor? The baker? The candlestick maker, if they had one? Why pick a woman at all, which would have been odd enough back then by itself, but especially a *fallen* woman? That's what she would have been called! And admit it, folks, that's what she'd be called by many of us today. A *fallen woman*." Brother Birdsong's voice had become strident. He looked around. David didn't think this called for a smile, but he gave a look of close attention. Again Brother Birdsong glanced their way for only a moment. "Here's what I think. I think that Jesus was there to lift people up. The mayor, the baker, they didn't need lifting up. He chose this sinful woman for his message, because she was the one who needed it most. And there's also a message in it for all of us! The message for all of us should be this:" He paused dramatically and looked around again, starting on his left and sweeping his eyes across to his right, to David's side of the church.

"No matter what you've done, no matter what you're *doing*, you can be forgiven. And not just that! You can even be a force for Good. Jesus didn't turn away the Woman at the Well, and he won't turn you away, either. He won't turn any of us away. All we have to do is say, enough. I'll drink no more from this well, this *worldly* well. I'm going to drink the Living Water."

Brother Birdsong looked down at the pulpit once more and turned some pages before him. The church was so quiet that the rustle of the paper could be heard. There was a strange, pleading tone in Brother Birdsong's voice that they were not accustomed to. It seemed to make everyone uncomfortable somehow. "And now," Brother Birdsong said at last, "turn in the hymnal to..." He stopped. After another long moment during which some uneasy fidgeting began to rise once more among the congregation, he turned toward Mrs. Birdsong, who sat at the organ. She frowned slightly at her husband, which was also unusual. "Hey," he said, "you know what? I know we generally save it for the end, but let's have *Just As I Am.*" Mrs. Birdsong hesitated just a moment, then put her hands on the keys and the music began.

After church that day, David remembered, Glenda seemed annoyed by Brother Birdsong's sermon. She called it a "lecture." David didn't think it was that bad, though he agreed that there had been a weird vibe that day. He just said, diplomatically, that well, maybe it hadn't been one of his best. Glenda cut him off. She said she had an idea. How about next Sunday they take a look at a new church with a new minister about whom she had heard very good things.

The church was called The Great Rock.

21

There was a smell of brimstone in the kitchen. Or possibly it was the bourbon.

David twitched back into the here and now to find Deion stamping in from the living room, speaking back over his shoulder. "—not my first priority right now, Jeremy!"

Jeremy followed, looking over his own shoulder back toward the television. "Second thought, it might just be his TV," he said. "Most people don't realize that the default chroma settings on these cheap LCDs are--"

"Please, Jeremy!" Deion rounded on him. "I really need to talk with David. Do you mind?"

"Why would I mind?" Jeremy replied, blinking innocently.

Deion sighed in frustration. "David, could we possibly..." He stopped, his eyes widening as he noticed the bottle on the table and the glass in David's hand. "Are you drinking liquor?"

"Yes," said David. "His name is Jack. I mean, its name is Jack. First name." He raised the glass to Deion and took a sip.

"I had no idea you drank," Deion said.

"Well, you know, I don't as a rule," said David. "But since my wife left me, and all her *boyfriends—*" he shrieked the word and both the other men flinched, "have started hounding my *every step*! I've reassessed some of my old habits! Or lack of habits." He gave a giggle that ended in a snort and took another drink.

Deion gave Jeremy a worried look. Jeremy shrugged helplessly. "David," Deion said, pulling out a chair and sitting down. "I understand that you are going through a deeply traumatic time, and I want you to know how much I sincerely regret my part in causing it."

"Which night was yours?" David asked. "Jeremy was Thursday and Blaney was Friday. When did she manage to squeeze you in?" David shuddered. "Oh God. What did I say?" He upended the glass.

Deion looked away. "I've been weak," he said, shaking his head and looking at the floor. "I hope that someday you can forgive me."

"Don't," said David, reaching for the whiskey bottle, "hold your breath. Or do. Yeah, go ahead. Hold your breath."

Deion watched David clumsily begin to mix another drink. "Like I said, I know you're hurting, and maybe I have no right to give you any advice. But I have to tell you something, and I hope you can listen to me. This is not the answer!" He leaned across the table. "I know what I'm talking about, David. There's something you are probably not aware of. I'm an alcoholic."

"No kidding?" said Jeremy. "That explains some things."

Deion turned on him. "What?"

"Nothing!" Jeremy backed away.

Deion turned back to David, gathering himself. "I haven't had a drink for three years and seven months. But before Jesus helped me put that bottle down, I almost ruined my life and the lives of those I loved. That," he pointed at the bottle, "is not an answer to any problem. You think it is at first, but then, before you know it, it *is* the problem. It's a road that only leads straight down, and I hate to see you start down that road."

David stopped, the glass halfway to his lips. He looked at it. Was Deion right? What was he doing, anyway? What was the point of this? He could try to blank out the world, to obscure reality, to anesthetize himself, but he wasn't changing anything. Reality would still be there. The pain would still be there. Maybe he was deliberately trying to hurt himself. To trade one pain for another. Was he trying to numb his mind, or to destroy it?

He set the glass down on the table and put a hand over his eyes, suddenly exhausted. Deion reached out, laid a hand on David's arm and said, "I think maybe we should pray. Don't you?" A tear fell from behind David's hand onto the tabletop. He nodded. Deion looked at Jeremy, who stepped forward. All three bowed their heads. "Heavenly Father," Deion began.

The back door opened and Rolly Blaney stepped inside. He was missing his hat, his hair was sticking up and his shirt was torn at one shoulder. There was a large bruise on the left side of his face and a smear of dried blood under his nose. He looked from David to the other two men and curled a lip.

"Jesus Christ. We getting the band back together?"

David picked up the glass and downed half its contents in a gulp.

22

Blaney pointed at David, showing a hand with scarred and bloody knuckles.

"Burkitt, you asshole. You fucked up my transmission."

He hooked the door with his heel and sent it slamming shut with a resounding crash. Bitsy the cat bolted from beneath the table, ricocheted like a pinball off the far wall and disappeared into the living room. Blaney walked toward the table. David recoiled in fear, but Blaney wasn't coming for him; he was coming for the bottle. David grabbed for it, too late. "Hey! That's–"

Blaney stepped to the counter and snatched up the glass from the drying rack, poured a slug into it and took a drink. He clunked the bottle down onto the counter. "Where's your bathroom?" he said. David pointed. "Down the hall. Left." Blaney, drink in hand, lumbered out of the room. His heavy tread thudded away. A door slammed.

"What's that maniac doing here?" Deion stage whispered.

David shrugged wearily. "He comes, he goes. He doesn't wait for invitations. Nobody waits for invitations."

"That man's crazy! He pulled a gun on me!"

"Oh yeah," said Jeremy. "I didn't get a chance to tell you that part. It was nuts."

"Nuts is right," said Deion. "I thought he was gonna shoot me! He's nuts, and he's a racist. It made him crazy just to think that a Black man and his—" Deion stopped. "I mean... I don't mean *his*..." He petered out under David's blank stare and looked down at the table. David rose, went to the cabinet, and retrieved the liquor bottle.

From the living room came a blare of music. Jeremy turned to look. "Oh, hey! The Save Tennessee special is starting. I guess Janie managed it all right. Man, those cameras at the Great Rock are first class. I wish we had those at the station." The music continued, a high-energy pop-rock blast, mixed with the noise of an audience. Jeremy leaned against the doorway to watch.

Deion looked at the bottle David now clutched protectively. "Don't forget what I told you, David."

"About what?" said David.

There was a bang, a crash, thudding footsteps, and Blaney re-appeared in the doorway, drying his face with a towel. His hair was less wild and the blood on his lip was gone, but there was nothing he could do about the bruise and the eye that was swelling toward shut. He clumped into the room, circled the table, pulled out a chair and fell into it heavily. He put the towel and his glass, now empty, on the table. With his good eye he gave Deion a look of withering disdain. "What are you doing here?"

"I came here to talk to David. To apologize."

Blaney grunted. "Apologize," he said. "You think that fixes any-thing?"

"It isn't about fixing it. It's about taking responsibility. Admit-ting the nature of my wrongs before God and those I've wronged, and making amends."

Blaney chuckled. "You a reformed drunk or something?"

"Whoa!" Jeremy said from the doorway. "How did you know that?" Deion glared at him.

"I recognize the bullshit," he said. "And let me guess. When you're through here, you'll go spill the beans to your wife, right?"

"That's right," Deion said defiantly. "Because the truth is the only–"

"Yeah, yeah, yeah. You'll make her miserable so you can feel better about yourself. I get it." He turned to David. "Awright," he said, "Where were we?"

"Were we?" said David. "What were we?"

Jeremy stepped into the room, peering at Blaney. "Holy moly," he said. "That guy did a number on your face!"

"What guy? Corley?" Blaney scoffed. "Kiss my ass! The day that pissant can lay a hand on me..." He apparently couldn't come up with anything unlikely enough to compare to that situation. "Corley is gonna wake up in the emergency room. If he wakes up."

"Then what happened?"

"The cop." Blaney reached out toward the bourbon bottle. "Gimme another shot of that."

"Get your own," said David.

"Cop?" said Deion.

"Yeah. He was a tough bastard. And that kevlar vest." He flexed his hand.

"You fought with a cop?"

Blaney gave him another hostile look. "I'm usually a Blue Lives Matter guy," he said pointedly, "but I didn't have time for a lot of disorderly conduct bullshit tonight. Quit screwing around and give me that!" David reluctantly relinquished the bottle, and Blaney poured another splash into his glass.

"Why didn't he shoot you?" said Deion, sounding a little disappointed. "He certainly would have shot *me*."

"He went for his taser," said Blaney, and he took a drink. "But it hung up on his belt or something. Let his guard down. Who cares? Let's get back to the subject at hand."

"Which is?" said David.

"You know which is. Where is she?"

David looked from one of their faces to the other, each staring back expectantly. He stood with the vague intention of objecting strongly to being questioned, only to find the kitchen floor to have tilted sharply, so he sat back down. He gripped the edge of the table to remain upright in his chair. "I don't know," he said.

"You want to know, don't you?" said Blaney.

"I'm not sure anymore!" David cried. He rubbed his face, which seemed to have gone numb. "I *thought* I wanted to know! But then I found out what I know now, and I don't even want to know *that* anymore! I don't know how much more knowing I can take! The more knowledge, the more sorrow! Ecclesiastes. You know?"

Blaney shook his head. "Aw shit," he grumbled. He picked up the cap and screwed it on the liquor bottle. "I *would* be dealing with the only damn Baptist in Christendom who can't hold his liquor." He reached over and dragged David's chair around to face him. "You know you want to know where she is. What she's up to. Admit it!"

David's eyes swam with tears. "Yes," he said. "I do want to know."

"All right then. You need to man up. Your woman left you. Could be worse. I've had a bunch leave me, and I can tell you from experience, quietly slipping away beats the hell out of some of the alternatives." He leaned back and picked up his drink, his voice dropping and his one good eye narrowing. "'Course, none of mine left me for somebody else."

"Until now, you mean?" said Jeremy, and Blaney gave him a look that made him hop back a step.

David eyed the cap on the bottle. "We don't really *know* that she left for–"

"Open your eyes, Burkitt!" Blaney cut in, and he moved the bottle farther away on the table. "Look how she was operating! Like some kinda damn master spy! Secret identities! Fake backgrounds and cover stories! And none of us had a fucking clue. All of us thought we were the only one. Mr. Right! Right?" Deion and Jeremy looked sheepish. Blaney nodded. "Right. Shit! We probably aint even all of 'em! Who knows how many there are?" David moaned and slumped

in his chair. "And now she goes dark. On all of us. All of us at once,"
Blaney went on. "And leaves doofus here a note, which blows her
cover! She's folded up her operation! She's in the wind! And there's
no God damn way she took off alone."

"She left a note?" said Deion. Blaney narrowed his eyes and
sipped his drink. "Don't look at me like that," Deion said. "It's like
you said. We're *all* in this, whatever this is. Whether you like it or
not." He pointed a finger. "And don't you start anything with me."

Blaney seemed to consider this a moment, then said, "I shouldn't
have pulled my pistol on you back there."

"You're darn right you shouldn't have," Deion replied with a nod.

"Man should never pull a gun unless he's gonna use it." Deion
started to say something, but stopped. Blaney set down his glass.
"Neither of you got any idea, I suppose? Where she might have
went, I mean." Jeremy and Deion looked at each other. "What I
figured."

"What's in the note?" Jeremy asked.

"Show 'em the note, Burkitt," Blaney ordered.

"It's private," said David, wiping his eyes.

"You already showed it to me! And it ain't like you got a lot of
secrets from this bunch."

David dug in his pocket for the paper. He laid the now ragged
sheet on the table, smoothed it out as best he could, and pushed it
across. Jeremy came over, and both he and Deion leaned over it to
read. Jeremy gave a low whistle. "Kind of..." he began.

"Terse," said Deion.

"Yeah, really...terse."

"'Things you can't give me,'" Deion read. He raised his eyes and
looked at David.

"What?" said David.

All three of the men looked at one another, then all looked at
David. "*What?*" he said.

"You got some kind of problem, Burkitt?" said Blaney. "In the husband department?"

David looked at him slackjawed. He looked at Deion and Jeremy. They all stared at him with a sort of tentative curiosity. "No!" David yelled. They didn't seem to buy it. "I don't!" They continued to stare. David pointed an accusing finger around the room. "She left all of you, too!"

That made them finally look away.

Blaney leaned wearily on the table. "Come on, Burkitt. Think about it! You must have some idea. Some clue to go on. Maybe you didn't see it at the time, but now that you know what's what."

Now that I know what's what? Did he really know what what was? What about it? Was there some clue among the myriad that had obviously escaped him that might yield some inkling as to where Glenda had gone and who with? *Glenda is gone.* Just re-thinking that thought wracked his body. He looked at the horrible note on the table. The buzzing started up again in his head. The voices from the TV in the next room seemed to swell in volume, though the words were unclear.

"I don't know. I can't think." He stood again and managed to stay on his feet this time. "I can't believe this is happening." He went to the counter and leaned on it, turned on the water in the sink and splashed some on his face. He grabbed the Coca-Cola-themed dish rag hanging from a bar on a cabinet door. "How could I be so blind? I think even Brother Birdsong knew something was going on. The Woman At The Well! And today he kept talking about *things*! *Things*! But I never for one second..." He rubbed his face with the towel, grimaced and threw it in the sink. It was sour.

"Birdsong?" said Blaney. "What about Birdsong? And what woman in a well?"

"*At* the well!" David leaned wearily on the counter, head drooping. "I went to see him today, to tell him Glenda had left. He didn't even seem surprised! He said it might even be for the best! I'm such an idiot."

Blaney rose and walked over to David. "Birdsong knew something? What exactly did he know?"

"I don't know. I left."

"Reverend Birdsong?" said Jeremy. "Uh, you don't think…"

"What?" David wheeled around, lost his balance and stumbled against Blaney. "No! There's no way!"

"OK," said Jeremy. "But, you know, up until today you would have said that about any of us."

"Get out of my way!" David pushed past Blaney and grabbed the liquor bottle. He removed the cap and threw it across the room. He poured the glass nearly full, not bothering with the mixer this time.

"Don't seem likely," Blaney said, but he didn't sound completely convinced. "Either way though, if he wasn't surprised like you said, then he must know something. And we got nothing else to go on."

When David finished coughing off his first gulp of straight bourbon he choked out, "What are you saying?"

"I'm saying let's go see Birdsong. See what he knows."

"Now?"

"No, next week. Yes, now! Where does he live? Or do you reckon he'll be at the church? It's past seven o'clock." He didn't wait for an answer. "We'll try the church first. Whose piece of shit is that out there in the driveway?"

"It's a Hyundai," said Jeremy, "and it's only three years old."

"You drive. They're sure to have a BOLO out on my truck. Also, Dale Bonehead, Junior here about fried the transmission."

"I'm going, too," said Deion, standing up.

"I'm taking my bottle," said David, clutching it to his breast with one hand, glass in the other.

"Jesus," Blaney muttered. "Whatever. Let's go." He strode across the room and headed for the front door.

"Is this a good idea?" said Jeremy.

"Decidedly not," said Deion. "But I think we better keep an eye on that maniac."

"Come on, God damn it!" Blaney shouted from the next room.

Jeremy and Deion made for the front door, and David shuffled after them. Entering the living room, he paused in front of the television. Reverend Dumond's handsome face filled the screen. "We are a Christian people," he said in his rich, melodious tones, "and ours is a Christian land. Shall we keep it so?" An unseen crowd gave an enthusiastic affirmation. "I'm asking you at home as well," he went on, gazing into the camera and therefore into David's eyes. "Will you help us keep it so? Every bit of help you can give, no matter how small, will support us in this work. Just call the number on your screen, or visit www dot–"

"Burkitt!" Blaney yelled from the front porch. David turned from the television, stumbled to the door and through it, pausing to clumsily, hands full, pull it closed behind him.

"While you're doing that," said Dumond on the television, "let's have a few moments of inspirational music from The Great Rock's rising star!" He made a sweeping gesture and stepped aside as the camera pulled back to show the stage. Music arose. The phone number and website remained at the bottom, but the image dissolved to a figure in silhouette, the lights backlighting it transformed into multi-colored, twirling stars by a camera filter Jeremy would have died for. The shadowy hand raised a microphone as the introduction led into the first verse. As a spotlight irised open, the figure began to sing.

Bitsy the cat came cautiously down the hallway from the back of the house into the living room, looking around.

She recognized that voice.

23

There was a great deal of jostling, complaining and, from Blaney, blasphemy, as they worked out who would sit where in Jeremy's three-year-old Hyundai. David concentrated mainly on not spilling anything from his glass. Finally, Jeremy at the wheel and Blaney riding shotgun, Deion and David in the back, the car backed out and drove away down the street.

None of them noticed another car parked on the street, which came to life and followed them.

24

"What's with all the cars?"

There was a lot of activity at the side door of First Baptist. People were coming out, getting into cars, pulling out of the lot. Lights were on in some of the windows. Jeremy stopped at the corner of the building.

"Choir practice, maybe?" ventured Deion.

"Whatever it is," said Jeremy, "looks like it's over. Everybody's leaving."

"Question is," said Blaney, "is one of the cars Birdsong's?"

"Parsonage is just around the corner," said David sluggishly. The rocking and stuffy warmth on the ride over had nearly lulled him to sleep. "They walk."

"All right. We'll have to check it out. Back up and park there in front."

"There's spaces by the side door now," said Jeremy.

"Too tight around here." Blaney frowned at the building. "Out front gives us a clear line of egress."

"Egrets?" mumbled David.

"Egress!" Blaney snapped. "A line of retreat."

"Retreat?" said Deion. "From what?"

"You never know. Pull over there!"

Deion laughed. "Are you expecting some kind of Baptist ambush?"

Blaney turned in the seat to look at him. "You never know," he repeated.

"My God," Deion murmured.

Jeremy backed the car around and stopped. Blaney leaped out. Deion, still muttering, opened his own door. David had more trouble getting his door open, partly because a car door handle had suddenly become a surprisingly complex mechanism, and partly because, though he had accidentally dropped his now-empty glass into the floorboard, he would not loosen his grip on the now nearing-empty liquor bottle. The four walked in the yellow glare of a streetlight toward the large double doors of the church, Blaney out in front. When he reached the doors, he gave one a tentative pull. It opened. He gave a thumbs up.

"Wait a minute," said David.

"What?"

"This is a church!"

"No shit. So?"

David looked at the bottle in his hands. "I can't take this in there."

"Then leave it!" Blaney opened the door wide and waited.

David looked around. There were two large ferns in planters on either side of the door. He went to one and carefully placed the liquor bottle on the ground beside it. He had to brace himself against the wall when he stood up again. He looked at Deion, pointed at the bottle. "Don't let me forget where I put that!"

Deion sighed, took David's arm and steered him toward the doorway.

The sanctuary was dark except for a row of small spotlights shining on the paintings on the wall behind the choir loft. The door to the hallway next to the organ was propped open and light poured through it. The quiet of the space was almost palpable, but there was a barely audible murmur of voices from farther back in the building. The four of them made their way down the center aisle toward the pulpit. David moved slower and slower, stumbling occasionally, not taking his eyes off the paintings spotlighted on the wall. When he reached the front row, he sat heavily down at the end of the pew next to the aisle.

Blaney went to the doorway and peeked up the hall. When he saw where David had landed, he said, "Leave him there." He noticed a wastebasket next to the organ, picked it up, brought it over and set it in near David. David looked at him quizzically. "It's gonna happen," said Blaney. "Might as well be ready for it." He moved back to the hallway. "Let's go!"

"What are we doing, exactly?" asked Deion.

"Looking for Birdsong!" Blaney said impatiently. "Remember?"

"What do you think he'll tell you?"

"Don't know 'til I ask him."

"I don't feel right just busting in on whatever they're doing back there," said Deion.

"Then stay here!" Blaney started down the hallway. They watched him go.

"What should we do?" Jeremy asked.

"I don't know." Deion looked around as though an answer might be floating somewhere nearby. "He's really starting to scare me. Why is he so hell bent on doing this right this minute?"

"He wants to help David find his wife, doesn't he?"

"Wife!" David mumbled.

Deion lowered his voice. "Jeremy, come on! Do you really think Rolly Blaney gives a damn about David?"

Jeremy considered. "Well..."

"He's crazy to find Glenda!" Deion whispered. "Why? What does he plan to do then?"

Jeremy looked up the hallway. "Oh man," he whined. "This is really messed up." Blaney, after creeping along one wall like a ninja infiltrating the Emperor's palace, disappeared around a corner. As he did so he laid a hand on the pistol in the holster on his belt. Jeremy turned to Deion. "You think maybe that cop did some damage to his head?"

"That man's head damage goes *way* back." Deion came to a decision. "Come on. We better follow him. In case there's trouble." He started up the hallway.

Jeremy hesitated. "Really? What kind of troub–"

"Come on!" Deion snapped. Jeremy groaned another low, "Oh, man," and followed.

David was alone in the sanctuary.

He leaned back. The images on the lighted wall went slowly in and out of focus, a strange phenomenon he attributed to maybe something wrong with the lighting. The wall featured a triptych of paintings of the life of Jesus. The painting on the left was of the infant, people and animals gathered around the glowing manger– this Bethlehem barn being equipped with a spotlight, apparently. On the right was the dark entry to the empty tomb, its stone door rolled away, some vaguely biblical-looking people gawping at it in amazement, an ethereal Christ looking down from the clouds above. The painting in the center was the largest, as it was actually a screen designed to cover the opening behind which was the clear, plexiglas tank which could be filled with water to baptize the faithful. The image on the screen depicted Jesus' own baptism. He stood waist-deep in the Jordan River, John the Baptist, fur-clad and looking a little like a caveman, at his side. The sky above was filled with a white light that shone down in rays, a dove sweeping down from it, bringing the news that Jesus was God's son, in whom he was well pleased. When a baptism was being performed and the lights were switched properly—bright inside, dark outside—it would become semi-transparent, the minister and subject visible, the dove seeming to swoop down on them as it had on Jesus. It was a nice effect.

Well pleased, David thought. *Matthew. Good Stuff in Matthew.*

David remembered his own trip as a teenager up the little, cramped stairway behind the choir loft, wearing a white robe over his swim trunks, to where Brother Birdsong, the new, young pastor at First Baptist, looking nothing like a caveman, stood in the tank of water. He remembered how he felt the eyes of the congregation, invisible in the darkness beyond that screen. How Brother Birdsong had smiled and reached out a hand. The steps down. The coolness of the water. The words spoken over him. Going under and knowing that when he came up again he would be a different person. "Well pleased," he mumbled, tears welling up in his eyes. How he wished he could do that again. Wash everything away. Or maybe just stay down there in the water this time. Not come up at all.

David felt rather than heard someone approaching down the aisle behind him. For a second he thought it was the others returning, then he remembered they had left in the other direction. He quickly wiped away the tears and tried to sit up straighter, preparing to attempt to present himself as perfectly calm, in control, and, above all, *sober* to whomever this turned out to be. He continued to look straight ahead as though perhaps he had just dropped in to admire the paintings.

Whoever it was stopped next to his pew and slightly behind him. Should he turn and look, or go on pretending to be enthralled by the art and unaware of their presence? The pause grew longer, and David grew more nervous. Finally there was movement, followed by the *clunk* of something being set down on the arm of the pew next to him. David turned his head to look.

It was his bottle of Jack Daniels.

25

The voices became louder and clearer as Blaney eased down the hallway. The earlier crowd had dispersed, but someone was still there in what, according to a sign above the door, was a Sunday School classroom. He recognized Birdsong's voice saying something indistinct, then a woman insisted that someone take the last of the cupcakes. Blaney reached the doorway, moved away from the wall, and stepped into the room. The people in the room turned to look at him.

"You have got," he said, "to be shitting me."

The chairs in the room were disordered, but generally faced a lectern near one wall. There was a table against the opposite wall with the remains of refreshments. It might have been the scene of a typical Baptist prayer group or possibly a book club meeting, except for the four people, three men and one woman, standing near the podium in close conversation with Brother Birdsong. The woman, small, young, wore a long, loose, blue dress and a gray scarf wrapped about her head and neck. One of the men was bearded and wore a robe-like, white outfit and a small, round cap. The other two men, Blaney noted, were dressed like "normal" people, a young man in jeans and sweater and an older man with a mustache in a sport coat and necktie, but both of them were, like the other two, undeniably *swarthy*.

Brother Birdsong was in the act of shaking the older man's hand. He looked at Blaney, dumbfounded. The headscarf woman gasped and grabbed the arm of the young man in the sweater. "He has a gun!" she said. The group tensed. Blaney glanced down at his hand, which he had rested automatically and absentmindedly on the butt of his pistol. Rather than remove it, he gripped the gun tighter. "Damn right I do," he said. "You ever hear of the Second Amendment?"

Brother Birdsong stepped between Blaney and the others. "Everyone relax! It's all right!" He sounded about seventy-five percent certain he was telling the truth. "What are you doing here, Mr. Blaney?"

"Wanted to talk to you about something. I didn't know you was holding a meeting of your...cell, or whatever it is." He still had not taken his hand off his pistol or his eyes off the four strangers.

Birdsong laughed ruefully. "You beat everything, Mr. Blaney. As a matter of fact, we've been having a little community meeting, my friends here and several others. Sort of like the one you and I attended earlier. About tomorrow's...festivities." He pointed at Blaney's sidearm. "Do you mind?"

Blaney moved his hand from his pistol, but only far enough to hook his thumb in his belt. Mrs. Birdsong popped up in front of him with a concerned look. Blaney recoiled. "My goodness, that eye looks terrible. What happened to you?"

"It ain't nothing," said Blaney uncomfortably.

"Well, you should put something on it. Cupcake?" She held out a plate.

A voice piped up behind Blaney. "Oh wow, are those carrot cake?"

Deion and Jeremy were in the doorway, Jeremy eying the plate of cupcakes greedily. Mrs. Birdsong muttered, "Pardon," stepped around Blaney and held it out to them. "They sure are! Homemade." Jeremy said, "Thanks!" enthusiastically and took one. Mrs. Birdsong extended the plate to Deion, but he made a polite gesture of "no thanks."

"Well," said Brother Birdsong, "you seem to be heading a delegation. Come in, gentlemen." Deion and Jeremy stepped into the room. Deion nodded awkwardly to the others. Jeremy was too focused on his cupcake to take much notice.

The man in the suit jacket walked over. "So you are Mr. Rolly Blaney?" he said, the slight lilt of an accent in his voice. "I'm glad to meet you. I am Mohammed Bahri." He extended a hand.

"Charmed," said Blaney, ignoring the hand. "Like I said, I come to talk to Birdsong."

"Of course," said Bahri, lowering his hand. "We won't keep you from your business." He turned to his three companions. "This is the man. The one who got those people at the big church all stirred up." The three looked at Blaney with new curiosity, like people encountering an unknown species in a zoo.

"I didn't stir 'em up," said Blaney. "You done that. All I done was tell 'em about you."

"I'm sorry, Dr. Bahri," said Brother Birdsong. "I had no idea he was–"

"It's quite alright, Reverend!" Bahri assured him. "It's good to put a face with the name."

Blaney, ever annoyed to one extent or another, became extra annoyed. "Have to excuse everybody for getting bent out of shape," he said sharply. "Folks 'round here ain't used to having a bunch of A-rabs around."

"Blaney!" Brother Birdsong snapped.

"Oh, not everyone is 'bent out of shape,'" said Dr. Bahri, his smile not faltering. "I'm Egyptian, by the way. Or rather, I was. I'm an American now for quite a while."

"Uh huh," Blaney said flatly.

"Mr. Blaney," Bahri said, becoming serious, "may I ask you something?"

"What?"

"Correct me–and forgive me–if I am wrong, but I get the feeling that you yourself don't hold any strong religious convictions."

Blaney laughed. "You can say that again."

"Then why," Bahri said, his voice showing his genuine puzzlement, "do you feel so strongly about this? About us? Why go to such lengths to, you claim, protect...from what, I'm not sure...a Faith you don't even hold?"

Blaney stared at Dr. Bahri, who raised his eyebrows questioningly, then he looked around to find that the others in the room were all also awaiting his answer. "How about you?" he said. "Big believer, are you?"

"I am a believer, yes," said Bahri.

"You, too, right, Birdsong?"

Brother Birdsong sighed. "Yes, Mr. Blaney, of course I am."

"Yeah, but you don't believe the same thing." Blaney nodded. "You wanna know *why* you two believe what you believe?" He did not wait for a reply. "OK then, I'll tell you. You believe what you believe because a long time ago in one place or another a bunch of fellas got together and killed everybody who believed different." Blaney hitched his belt up and hung both thumbs in it, spread his feet apart. "What this business is about," he proclaimed, "is *power*. Power! Plain and simple. You ever see where the Pope lives? You don't get a hundred-acre palace and your own private bank by just loving Jesus. And you sure as shit don't get it by turning your other cheek. Power!" He strode into the room, looking around disdainfully at the books on the shelves, the posters on the wall. "Mohammed or Jesus or even Joseph Smith–" He stopped, raised a finger. "Did you know the Mormon Church owns two *million* acres of real estate?" He resumed stalking the room. "Jesus, Mohammed, whoever. That's just the label on the bottle. The booze inside the bottle is *power*. Somebody's gonna have it, and whoever has it will step on them that don't. You're gonna be the stepper or you're gonna be the steppee." He jerked a thumb toward Deion. "That's the reason we gotta keep *them* down."

"*What?*" Deion cried.

Blaney went on. "Dumond, now? Dumond gets it," he said. "Dumond knows what it's really all about. That's why Dumond has three TV stations, four radio stations and a thousand-seat theater, and Birdsong here preaches every Sunday to a dozen geezers, and half of them with their hearing aids turned off."

Blaney turned to address Bahri directly. "Power. Here, we got it. You don't. And I want to keep it that way." He gave a rueful shake of his head. "I'll admit we got a disadvantage, though. Your side," he waved a hand at Bahri's three companions, "will strap on a bomb and blow theirselves up. Ours may not show up if it's threatening rain."

Blaney appeared to have finished his disquisition. The room was silent for a long moment. Deion seethed. Jeremy had forgotten to chew his cupcake, and choked slightly. Bahri shook his head and looked at his stunned companions. "Well," he said, "I asked."

He turned to Brother Birdsong. "Thank you again for all your help, and we'll see you in the morning. Shall we go?" The three others shook hands and offered quiet farewells to Reverend and Mrs. Birdsong, both of whom mumbled apologies and were reassured in turn. At the door, the young woman turned and looked at Blaney. "I have heard of the Second Amendment," she said. "Have you ever heard of the First?" The young man in the sweater put a hand on her shoulder, and they continued out the door.

"Some company you're keeping, Birdsong," said Blaney.

Brother Birdsong shook his head in weary disbelief. "You have some gall, Mr. Blaney. Barging in here to my church and harassing my guests, strutting around with your blasphemous speechifying like some kind of cornpone Mussolini. Lord help us, man. Were you raised by wolves?"

26

The bottle sat at David's elbow like an accusation, and he was not sure what to say or do. A machine gun burst of excuses and denials ran through his foggy mind, much like once when he was eight years old and broke a vase. *What's that? I don't know anything about that. The dog did it!* He could barely think and what he did think sounded unconvincing to him. Nothing came out. After a moment, the shadowy figure moved, a hand appeared, grasped the bottle and lifted it again. David's eyes widened. The fingernails on the hand were long and orange.

Laura, Channel 38's don't-call-me-receptionist, walked around the front of the pew, watching him intently. He watched her back, in confusion and with a certain amount of disbelief. She wore the same yellow dress she had worn earlier at the TV station, but her necklace was gone now. *Otherwise, I would have heard her clanking,* he thought. Her dark, red hair was somewhat disheveled. She wore a slight, sardonic grin. Still having said nothing, she sat down on the pew next to him. She held the bottle up and regarded its contents, then looked at him from the corner of her eye.

"Do you mind?"

Her voice seemed to David at least half an octave lower than usual. He shrugged, not knowing exactly what it was that he wasn't minding. Laura tipped the bottle up, took a drink, grimaced, blew out a breath and drew a deep one in. "I went to your house," she said. "To see you. But *they* were there." She jerked her head toward the hallway door. Her tone seemed to evince disapproval of his choice of companions. "Saw you leave. Followed you here." She held the bottle out to him. He shook his head, still not certain he wanted to admit ownership. "Those *men*," she said, the word heavy with contempt, "They don't know, David. They don't know. Not like we do."

"Know?" he said.

Laura took a deep breath. "Glenda," she said, "She..." She looked at him. There were tears in her eyes. The way the "s" in that word had slurred led David to speculate that maybe his was not the first bottle she had partaken of this evening. "How could she do it, David?"

David tried to sit up straighter, but immediately slid back into a slouch. "You... You know about it?"

"Of course I know about it!" She leaned back against the pew. "Glenda, Glenda," she said to the ceiling, then she took a deep breath and sighed it out again. "I would never have thought I could love a woman...that way. Until I met her." She took another drink.

David considered this statement and gauged with some interest his mental response to it. Just a few hours earlier, he thought, how puzzled he would have been! He would not have had a clue what she was talking about. *That way? What way?* And when it was finally, laboriously made clear just what way "that way" was, he would have gone into a state of shock. Those were the days! When he could still be shocked! Now, it seemed, even this couldn't do it. Maybe it was the numbing effect of the liquor, but he thought it just as likely that he was simply shocked out. After the events of the day, maybe there was just no more shock left in him.

"She showed me so many things. Things about myself," Laura went on dreamily. "About..." She put a hand to her throat, ran it down over her breasts and torso. "About my body." She turned to him. "You know the things she can do."

"Uh huh," said David. He reached for the bottle, took a swallow, coughed, and choked out, "She's a pip, all right." He felt another swallow was called for.

"Them!" Laura gave another scornful nod toward the hallway. "They were just playthings. All of them were!"

"All of them?" said David.

"But you and I... We meant something. Something *real*!" She stifled a sob. "Or I thought we did! How could she do it?" she wailed. "Just suddenly leave us? Both of us! For *him!* And a three-line note. That's all I rated. How about you?"

"Four," he said, "Not counting the signature. But who do you mean she—" He stopped. "Wait a minute. You got a note, too?"

"Nobody understands, David," she said, turning toward him, sliding closer, one arm on the back of the pew. "Nobody can *really* understand but you and me. That's why I came looking for you. We share a bond." She laid a hand, fingers splayed, on the part of her chest that had earlier been armored by the necklace. Her expression changed, became intense. Her breathing grew ragged and quick. For a moment David thought she was going to sneeze. Instead, she snatched the bottle from his hand, reached around and set it down on the pew behind her. "What–?" David began, then he discovered that he was not entirely shocked out after all.

Laura swung herself up onto one knee and threw the other across his lap. She sat down astride him, grabbed his head and kissed him so violently as to be painful. He instinctively grabbed at her with both hands, to find that her short, possibly-a-bit-too-young-for-herself dress had ridden up on her hips. With that he learned that he actually had quite a bit of remaining shock left–a particularly rich vein of it, in fact. Laura, it seemed, did not wear underwear.

She pressed her forehead to his. "We can make it, David," she panted, her breath redolent of bourbon and peppermint. "Help me. And I'll help you." She kissed him again, moving her body, grinding herself against him. Her tongue darted into his mouth.

David began to feel many things he had never felt before, at least not in the way he was feeling them now. He felt warm flesh under his fingers. He felt the world begin to spin around him. He felt his body begin to react of its own accord. Then, with a jolt, he remembered where he was. He pulled away. "Laura! Stop!" he gasped. "Look where we are! We can't do this here!"

She looked into his eyes, breathing deeply. "Where, then?" she whispered.

David looked down. Laura's not inconsiderable bosom was pressed against him, and at chin level lay the deep fissure between her breasts, closing and opening as she breathed in and out. As he stared into that abyss, she started moving against him again, slowly.

"I know a place," he said.

27

Mrs. Birdsong laid a hand on her husband's arm to calm him.

"Take it easy, *Bird-song*," said Blaney. "How did I know you was running a mosque nowadays?"

"What do you want?" Reverend Birdsong demanded angrily. "All of you! What are you doing here?" He reached over and snatched the last cupcake from his wife's plate.

"I'm sorry, Reverend Birdsong," Deion said sorrowfully. "We didn't mean to–"

"We want to know what you know about Glenda Burkitt," Blaney cut in. He plopped onto one of the folding chairs, crossed his arms and waited expectantly.

Brother Birdsong stopped peeling the paper from the cupcake. "Glenda Burkitt?" he said. "What about her?"

"What I just said. She's gone. What do you know about it?"

"What on Earth makes you think I know anything about it?"

"Burkitt says so."

"David?" Brother Birdsong looked from Blaney to the other two men.

"Have you seen him?" Mrs. Birdsong asked. "How is he?"

"He ain't feeling no pain," Blaney said drily. "You gonna answer my question? Or maybe you don't want to talk about it in front of the little woman?"

"Did he just call me 'little woman?'" It was Brother Birdsong's turn to pat his wife's arm placatingly.

"Just what is it that I'm supposed to–" Brother Birdsong stopped. He put his cupcake back on his wife's plate. "You know what? I've had just about enough of you, Blaney. Come to your point if you have one, or get out of here.”

Deion stepped forward. “It’s just that David said when he told you about Glen– About his wife disappearing, you didn’t seem surprised. Like maybe you already knew something.”

“I don’t need no translator, Mullins,” Blaney said darkly.

“Well, yeah, you kinda do!”

“Hold on a minute,” said Brother Birdsong. “Why are *you* asking about this? How is Glenda Burkitt’s whereabouts any business of yours?” There was a moment of silence, awkward on Deion’s part, sullen on Blaney’s. Jeremy, intent on finishing the final crumbs of his cupcake, noticed the quiet and wondered what he just missed.

Reverend and Mrs. Birdsong looked at each other again, and at that moment there passed between them that sudden, mystical, semi-psychic, comprehensive grasping of the gist similar to that which David had encountered earlier that day. After looking at each other with mirrored expressions of growing shock, they looked again at Blaney. “Good Lord,” said Brother Birdsong. They looked at Deion and Jeremy. Deion, unable to hold their gaze, looked at the floor. Jeremy looked like an icing-smeared deer in headlights.

“Oh come now!” said Mrs. Birdsong in amazement. “Not *all* of you, surely?”

Blaney uncrossed his arms. Their psychic get-the-gist trick unnerved him as much as it had David. “What say we just stick to the subject?”

“Glenda Burkitt,” Brother Birdsong began, carefully choosing his words, “is...”

“I’ll tell you what she is,” said Mrs. Birdsong. “She’s nothing but a–” Brother Birdsong managed to cut her off, but she stood seething.

“Glenda,” Brother Birdsong went on, “is a complicated and troubled...” He looked from one of the three men to the other and shook his head, "...*deeply* troubled woman. We've been aware of that for a while, I'm sad to say. And in retrospect, I suppose I should have talked to David about it before it came to this."

Deion stepped forward, distressed. "You're saying she...approached you, too?"

Brother Birdsong looked hurt. "Is that so hard to–" He shot a glance at his wife and stopped.

"He told her 'no,'" Mrs. Birdsong said imperiously, "And it begins to look like he's the only man who ever did!' Her accusing stare was so strong that even Blaney had to look down at his hands.

Brother Birdsong cleared his throat. "The point is," he said, "I have no idea where she is. And anyway, any discussion I had with David about her, or any other topic for that matter, is between him and myself. Private."

"What?" said Blaney, getting to his feet. "Baptists doing confessions these days? Or are you Catholic now, too? Catholic! Moslem! Any denominations you ain't got covered?"

"I think we're done, Mr. Blaney," said Brother Birdsong coldly. "Unless you'd like this last cupcake, we have no more business. Good night."

"Wait," said Mrs. Birdsong. "What about David? He was in a terrible state this afternoon. Did you say you've seen him? Talked to him?"

"Sure," said Jeremy. "He's here. Is anybody–"

"Here?" said Brother Birdsong. "Where?"

Jeremy pointed, first in the wrong direction and then, correcting himself, toward the sanctuary. "Out there. In the church. Anybody gonna take that last cupcake...?"

28

The sanctuary was empty.

"He was right here," said Deion, pointing to the front pew, the wastebasket standing nearby. The five of them stood just inside the doorway near the organ. Jeremy brought up the rear, putting away the final crumbs of the final cupcake.

"He's gotta be around somewhere," said Blaney. "He could barely walk."

"The man's never had a drink in his life!" said Brother Birdsong. "I can't believe you let him get drunk!"

"Let him!" said Blaney. "I'd like to seen somebody stop him."

"I tried," said Deion.

"Yeah, he did. I heard him." said Jeremy, licking his fingers. "Did you know that Deion is an al–"

"Jeremy!"

"Look in all the rows," said Mrs. Birdsong. "He may be lying on one of the pews." She started up the central aisle, looking left and right.

"Too dark in here," said Blaney. Brother Birdsong walked over to a row of switches on the wall next to the door. He flipped two and lights high up near the ceiling came on, illuminating the pews.

"David?" Mrs. Birdsong called. "Are you–" She stopped, listening.

"What–?" Brother Birdsong began, then he heard it, too.

They all heard it.

Each of them began to turn slowly around, triangulating, trying to locate where the sounds were coming from. Gradually they all ended up facing the front of the sanctuary. They each began to try to imagine what those sounds could be, because there was clearly no way they could possibly be what they obviously were.

"You gotta," said Blaney, "be shitting me."

Then, to his everlasting regret, Brother Birdsong turned and flipped the little set of switches beneath the stick-on label that read, "BAPTISTRY."

29

When he was a young man, not long after his baptism in fact, David developed appendicitis. Prior to taking him into surgery they gave him a shot of something which left him groggy and made it difficult for him to think straight. Rolling into the operating room, he began to worry about the possibility that he might die during the operation. The thing that bothered his drug-addled mind was not death itself so much as the thought that if death did come, he would be unconscious and therefore unable to tell whether he was dead or simply still asleep. He tried to ask the masked, upside-down man at the head of the operating table about it, but "How will I be able to tell?" came out, "Hobble hi bebble bell?" The man did not reply; he just put a different kind of mask over David's nose and mouth. As consciousness slipped away, he consoled himself with the realization that he surely would know if he had died, because if so, he would wake up in Heaven. Heaven would be all white and shiny. That would be the giveaway. When he awoke a while later to find himself staring at a blue ceiling, he knew he must have survived.

Now David jerked awake and was surprised to find that apparently Hell is white and shiny, too. All he could see was whiteness and shininess, and when he tried to move, he became awash in pain. Not a particular, localizable pain, like a headache or a sore leg; this was a non-specific, all-encompassing *environment* of pain, pain that permeated everything like a magnetic field. And not just physical pain–if anything, the physical was actually the lesser pain. Consciousness brought a wave of anguish and panic. He did not know where he was or what had happened, yet was gripped by an ironclad certainty that *something* had happened, and it was something unspeakably awful, something he couldn't quite remember, and did not want to, but he feared he would, and he dreaded it. Also, his mouth felt as though it was full of kerosene-soaked flannel.

The whiteness filling his vision began to coalesce into an object, but one which he could not readily identify. His awareness of space began to resolve itself such that he could tell he was lying on his side on a hard surface. His awareness of time, however, remained so fuzzy as to be incomprehensible. He knew neither where he was nor when he was.

He tried to lift his head, which turned out to be a terrible mistake. He discovered an excruciating crick in his neck, the pain of which radiated upward and through his skull like a lightning bolt. He tried to cry out, which made his throat feel like raw hamburger stabbed with a hot fork. This brought on a coughing fit, and each cough sent a shock of agony through him as though he were being rhythmically beaten with a baseball bat. An *aluminum* baseball bat.

He rolled onto his back to find shapes floating in the air above and to one side of him. They looked like fish. Blue and green fish. Was he underwater? Was he insane? No, to the first question at least. The fish were on a plastic shower curtain. A light fixture blazed painfully into his eyes, which had to indicate the ceiling of a room. This meant that he was lying on the floor of a room. The hard surface he felt with his right hand was the side of a bathtub. He carefully turned his head to the left. The shape that had filled his world upon waking and which now loomed above him was the white, porcelain bowl of a toilet. He was lying on the floor of a bathroom.

It was not his own bathroom. He was lying on the floor of an unknown bathroom. He tried to lift an arm and found something hindered him. He was tangled in a blanket of some kind. Assessing further, he determined that he seemed to be fully dressed with the exception of his shoes, one sock and his necktie. He closed his eyes to block, at least somewhat, the supernova brilliance of the ceiling light, and tried to puzzle out what was going on.

He remembered yesterday, if it was in fact yesterday, the worst–or at least the worst so far–day of his life. He recalled how the day had proceeded from one gut-wrenching revelation to another, each of which struck him anew now as he recalled it. The note. The Call. The meeting. Brother Birdsong's strange attitude. Rolly Blaney. That awful bar. Retreating to his empty home–empty but for that rotten cat!–only to find it no refuge, since everyone followed him there. He remembered...whiskey. Had he actually bought a bottle of whiskey? He had bought a bottle of whiskey! *My God*! What was he thinking?

The memories began to blur and break up there in his kitchen. He tried to follow the thread, but the effort was exhausting, and it inflamed the scorching pain in his head. He mostly remembered Blaney. Blaney, a demon who just kept hounding him. But the others were there, too. They took him somewhere, didn't they? Yes! To the church. First Baptist. That's right. He was in the church, and... There were images, disjointed, like flash photos taken in a darkened room.

Oh dear God, no.

He gasped, and his throat closed up again. The anguish and remorse he had felt upon waking washed over him once more, separate from and now much worse than the physical pain. Only this time the general feeling of dread had found its specific object. Bits of memory sizzled and jumped inside his head. He found that he couldn't breathe.

Water. He needed water.

He found he was cocooned in the scratchy blanket. It was wrapped around his waist and legs, and extricating himself seemed impossible. Using the rim of the bathtub, he pulled himself into a sitting position. The room spun around like a carnival ride. He smelled himself, a funk of spilled liquor and who knew what else. With sudden panic he realized that he was going to throw up. He barely managed to twist around and reach the toilet, its seat mercifully already raised. He heaved and heaved, his body spasming, but the process produced nothing but more agony. It finally stopped, and he lay his head on the rim of the bowl, mumbling, "Oh God, oh God."

Wherefor is light given to him that is in misery, and life unto the bitter in soul which long for death, but it cometh not?

That was the Book of Job. *No Good Stuff. No Good Stuff in Job.*

David sobbed, but his eyes were even too empty to produce tears. With an immense effort he shifted from leaning on the toilet to leaning on the cabinet next to the toilet. His legs were bound together by the blanket, but he managed to fold himself and with a mighty effort push/pull himself until his upper body lay on the countertop. The sink was at his right hand. He stuck his head as nearly into it as he could and turned on the tap. With the hand that wasn't holding him more or less upright he grabbed the faucet and directed the stream of water onto his face and into his mouth. Finally, gasping, he turned it off. It was then that he heard the tapping. He held his breath. The tapping came again. It came from the closed door at the end of the room. Someone was knocking on the door.

David was gripped by terror. The cold splash of water had sharpened his mind a little, and he now looked around the room again, searching for any clue as to who its owner might be. Frustratingly, the room was almost monastic in its simplicity. There were no decorations other than the colorful fish on the shower curtain. There was one toothbrush in a holder by the sink, a half-squeezed tube of toothpaste nearby. Sensitive teeth toothpaste, according to the label. What did that tell him? Nothing. There was a wicker clothes hamper that might hold some clues, but it was near the door and might as well have been on Mars.

The tapping came again. There seemed to be no avoiding it. He braced himself mentally as best he could and said, "Come in?" His voice was so raspy he didn't recognize it. The doorknob turned and the door opened slightly. Jeremy stuck his head in.

"Hi, Dave," he said. "You, uh... Feeling better? I hope?"

30

"See, with a drip coffee maker the water just sort of rushes through the coffee, but with a French press, the coffee *steeps* in the water. The same way you make tea! Well, not the same exactly, but the principle..."

David sat at the table in the tiny kitchenette in what had turned out to be Jeremy's apartment, the woolen blanket that had wrapped his legs now wrapped around his shoulders. Jeremy wore checked pajama bottoms and had his hair pulled back in a ponytail. His t-shirt this morning featured curvy script that spelled out, "Start Your Day With Jesus (and Coffee!)" Jeremy's process for making coffee resembled something more akin to alchemy. It also involved using an electric coffee grinder, which almost sent David back to the toilet.

"Here you go," he said, setting a cup down on the table. "See how you like it. It may be a little stronger than you're used to." David said, "Thank you," picked up the cup and sipped it gratefully. It was strong, but at that moment it couldn't be strong enough. He swallowed, and his stomach made a noise like a Benghal tiger having a nightmare.

"You want some toast?" Jeremy asked. "You ought to eat something. One thing's for sure: your stomach is definitely empty!" He rolled his eyes. "Sorry to leave you on the floor like that, but you didn't want to get too far from the pot."

David set the cup down carefully, his hands still shaky. "How did I get here?"

"You don't remember?"

"No."

Jeremy said nothing for a moment, covering his silence by moving to the refrigerator and taking out a tub of butter. "You don't remember..." he said, "any of it?"

"Well, I mean, I remember everyone coming to my house. And then we went to First Baptist...to see Brother Birdsong about...something. And then, while I was there..." He looked up at Jeremy, desperately hoping to see something in his face to tell him that what he thought happened hadn't actually.

Jeremy's expression sank any wispy hope David had remaining. "Yeah, well," Jeremy said, and he turned quickly away, moving to the counter to open a loaf of bread and put two slices into a toaster. "It was all...pretty messed up. First Rolly Blaney went off on a bunch of Muslims, which was weird. Him going off, I mean, but also seeing a bunch of Muslims in a Baptist Church in the first place. Then he kind of went off on Reverend Birdsong, too, and *he* got kind of P.O.'d. So now everybody was P.O.'d. Then we went looking for you, and..." He paused. "Boy, seeing Laura at work Monday is gonna be...awkward." He pushed down the lever and the bread disappeared.

"Oh God," David moaned.

"That's what she said!" Jeremy said brightly, then caught himself. "Oh. Sorry!"

"I can't believe it. I can't believe I did...that."

"I can't believe *she* did that!" Jeremy said. "I didn't think she even liked you. Or anybody else much, really."

David slumped over the table. "How can this have happened?"

"Because you were both drunk, probably," Jeremy said helpfully. "Boy, I'm sure glad I don't drink!"

"Neither do I! Or I didn't. I mean, I hadn't."

"You sure made up for lost time." David looked at him. "Sorry."

"How did I end up here?"

"Well, that gets kinda complicated." Jeremy leaned against the counter. "Things got a little wild there right after the lights came on. I mean... Holy Moly!" David moaned. "Mrs. Birdsong–"

"*She* was there?" David cried.

"Sure," said Jeremy, and chuckled. "Boy, you really don't remember, do you? She let out quite a yell. And I thought Reverend Birdsong might have a stroke. He turned the lights back off, which was a good idea, but I guess that made it harder for you two to get...untangled." David moaned again. "He and Deion went back there to bring you both out. You kept saying you were sorry, but you weren't making a lot of sense. Laura, though, she kept saying she *wasn't* sorry, and nothing mattered anymore, and you two have a 'bond' of some kind that we couldn't understand. I was blown away. Seriously. Like I said, I thought she didn't even like you!" The toast popped up behind him. He turned, gingerly snatched the slices out onto a saucer, got a knife from a drawer, took the saucer to the table and sat down. He began to butter the bread. "Everybody was talking and yelling and everything. Finally, we all went outside. Deion managed to get Laura to let him drive her home. Mr. Blaney went with them, I think because Laura was saying something about Glen– about your– You know. Glenda. I don't know how they were planning to get home after that. Me and Reverend Birdsong got you into my car. I was gonna drive you back to your house, but you were talking some pretty crazy stuff about your grief being heavy as the sands of the sea, and the arrows of the Almighty being in you, and about cursing God and dying. I didn't feel good about leaving you alone. So I brought you here. And you were... Well, I'm glad you feel better now. You had me kinda scared." He set the saucer with the buttered bread in front of David.

David never knew mortification could manifest itself as physical discomfort, but he felt it now, full blast. Yet something in the horrible story had caught his attention nonetheless. He mulled it over as he chewed and swallowed his first bite of toast, which fell into his stomach and sent reverberations through his system like a walnut dropped into a metal drum. "You say Laura was talking about Glenda? She said something to me, too. Earlier."

"Yeah, I didn't really get a lot of it because I was dealing with you. You were kind of hard to maneuver."

"Before she... Before we..." David covered his face with a hand. "In the *baptistry*! Oh my God!"

"Yeah," Jeremy agreed, and he gave a little whistle of amazement.

"She said something about Glenda leaving us for *him*."

"Leaving *us*?" said Jeremy.

David pretended not to notice that. The situation was complicated enough already. "She said 'left with *him*,' but she didn't say who *he* was."

"Maybe that's what she was talking about when they were getting her in the car. Whatever it was, it sure got Mr. Blaney's attention. What's his deal, anyway? I never met anybody so angry about everything. Deion felt the same way. He was scared Blaney might really do something."

"Do something?" said David.

"Yeah. To Glenda. If he found her."

David stopped chewing. The bread seemed to turn to ashes in his mouth.

"Well," Jeremy said, "It's almost eight. I'm gonna get dressed, and then I'll take you home. By then it will be time to go to the Thing."

"Thing?" David said around the toast.

"Yeah. You know! The Make Tennessee Safe for Christianity Thing. It's this morning, remember? I'll be shooting some video. Probably going to make a big special about it for the station. Nobody asked me to, but they'll be glad I did!" He stood.

"Jeremy, listen," David said, choking down the bread. "I want to thank you. For what you've done for me."

Jeremy looked at the floor, and around the edges of his beard David could see a blush rising. "Gee, Dave. Don't say that. Don't thank me! Really. I don't deserve it. You did something you regret, right? Well, I regret what I did, too. And I have no excuse."

David sighed. "I don't blame you, Jeremy. Not anymore. Everything is more complicated than I used to think. Things, and *people* are more complicated. More than I ever knew." There was a moment of silence. "And please don't call me Dave. Nobody calls me Dave."

"OK. Sorry." Jeremy started toward the bathroom, but stopped in the living area. "Oh!" He carefully lifted something from the coffee table and dropped it on the table in front of David. It was a twisted yellow strip of cloth. "I'm sorry about your tie. You had jammed the knot so tight I had to cut it off with scissors. You got it in...you know. The toilet and stuff."

David looked at it bleakly. "O.K.," he said. "Where are my shoes? And I think I left my phone at home, but did you see my keys?"

"I guess you left your shoes in the...where you were. Don't know about the keys. Maybe they fell out of your pockets when they were trying to...you know...get your pants back on."

David moaned and slumped forward onto the table.

O.K. then," Jeremy said nervously. "Oh!" He pointed at David's shoulders. "Just throw the afghan on the couch when you're done with it." He left the room.

David slowly sat up and picked up his coffee cup, but froze with it halfway to his mouth. He looked down at the woolen fabric draping his shoulders.

Afghan?

He bounced to his feet and tossed it aside. Luckily his coffee had cooled enough that it didn't scald him.

31

Jeremy's apartment was only ten minutes or so from his own house, but David was starting to drift off before they were halfway there. The coolness of the car window was soothing to his forehead, even if the vibrations were not. The main point of this position, however, was his hope that turning his head away and closing his eyes might discourage Jeremy from continuing to make light conversation. David wanted no more conversation, light or otherwise, with Jeremy or anyone else—conversation, with its seemingly inexhaustible cargo of unwanted revelations. He just wanted to get home, stand under his shower until the hot water ran out, then go to bed. Forever.

"Hey, Dave?" said Jeremy. "Sorry! David?"

Naturally. "Yes?"

"Should you really be all by yourself right now? Don't you have somebody you can go to? Family or somebody? So you don't get all...bummed out and stuff?"

"I'm already pretty bummed out, Jeremy," David said. "I don't know how I could be bummed much farther out."

"Yeah, but isn't there somebody?"

David considered. His parents had moved to Arizona two years ago when his father retired. His sister lived in Dallas. But even if they had been close by, how could he talk to them about this? In fact, the inevitability of eventually talking to them—or anybody else—about this was one of the top things he wanted to crawl into a hole and avoid. As for friends, he had some, certainly. But not that many and not that close.

I didn't need friends! I had Glenda!

He felt a bubble of self-pity rising, constricting his throat. Was there really nobody he could look to for help? For understanding? There had been, he realized. "Before," he said, "I could talk to Brother Birdsong." He choked. "But now I can never look him in the eye again." He sighed in misery, and an image of the previous night flashed into his mind. He thought of Mrs. Birdsong being present. A red-hot bolt of shame arced through him, so sharp that it produced an audible cry of pain.

"What is it?" asked Jeremy.

"Nothing," said David, pressing his head back against the glass. "Everything," he whispered.

"You got some Advil or something at home?" Jeremy asked. "Tylenol?" David did not reply. Jeremy snapped his fingers. "Hey, you know, you could talk to Reverend Dumond. Once he's through with the Thing. He's a pretty wise guy."

David thought about it. He found that he couldn't really imagine that scenario. He had had only a few one-on-one encounters with Reverend Dumond, and nothing about them led him to conjure an image of the man as sympathetic listener or helpful counselor. Charismatic preacher, yes, but... Reverend Dumond, with his steely confidence and rocklike certainty in the correctness of his own judgment, had never given the impression of having a lot of empathy for other peoples' weaknesses. Or was he being unfair again?

"Maybe," said David.

"And then, you know, there's always..." Jeremy twisted in his seat and plucked at his current t-shirt to point out the picture and message printed on it. This was yet another new one that David had never seen before. It featured Jesus from a renaissance painting sitting at a computer wearing a telephone headset beneath his halo. A logo on the computer monitor featured a cross and read,

"SUPPORT LINE 24/7." The caption: "Good News! I'm Here to Help!"

"Watch the road!" said David. There *was* that. *Keep Calm and Trust Jesus.* A lot of Good Stuff in the New Testament was about staying calm through fiery trials. But what he was going through now had a distinctly Old Testament feel. And even though Jesus must have forgiven a lot of worse people than him for even worse things, David was so ashamed of his actions of the night before that he wasn't sure he even had the nerve to pray about them.

What he really wanted was the answer to the one question that everyone asked, but that never received a clear answer no matter how hard one prayed. *Why?* Why him? Why *this?* Was it some sort of punishment? He tried to inventory his past sins, but he couldn't find any—prior to those of the previous night, anyway, he thought with a shudder—that he felt would remotely rate what he found himself going through. Or was considering himself so without sin itself a manifestation of sin? The sin of Pride. Would God really send this level of havoc just to take David Burkitt down a notch or two? For that matter, was believing that he was so *bad* as to deserve God's wrathful attention just as prideful as thinking he was too *good* to rate God's wrathful attention? He rolled his head against the cool glass. *A guy can't win.*

Or maybe God was just doing it to him on a bet, like He did with Job.

"Weird," said Jeremy. "Deion's car's still here." David raised his head. They had arrived at his house. Once again, he was struck with that feeling of dislocation; it was his house, but no longer his life. And yes, Deion's blue Nissan was in the drive behind his own car, seemingly unmoved from the night before. The sight of it and the echo of the previous evening that came with it gave David a chill. Jeremy pulled into the drive.

"Thank you for the ride." David opened his door.

"Don't you think it's weird?" Jeremy said, pointing at the car in front of them. "I wonder how Deion got home? You think Blaney's truck is still back there, too?"

David stopped halfway out of the car. Blaney had hidden his truck from view around back. Surely it wasn't still there? He had thought getting home would somehow end the nightmare, or at least this phase of the nightmare. He went pale and slumped back onto the car seat.

"You sure you're O.K.?" Jeremy asked. "I have a little time. Do you want me to come in with you and–"

"No!" David's head whipped around and his neck let out a clearly audible *crack.* He choked back a cry of pain and said, "Not necessary! You've done enough. I'm just going to..." He stopped and listened. "Did you hear that?"

"What?"

David had heard, or thought he heard, a thumping sound. He listened for another moment. Nothing. He began once more to lever himself out of the car. "Nothing. I thought I heard a—" It came again. Definitely a rhythmic thumping, followed this time by what sounded like a distant, muffled voice. "Turn the car off a minute," he said.

Jeremy turned off the engine and they both sat quietly. After a moment it came again. A low, *thump thump thump,* followed by an unintelligible voice, distant and muffled.

"What the heck?" said Jeremy, and he opened his door. They both got out of the car and walked around to the front bumper. They stopped and listened again. The sound came again, louder now, and its source became obvious. They turned and looked at the trunk of Deion's car. "Sounds like somebody's in there!" Jeremy said to David. He leaned toward the car and called louder, "Is somebody in there?"

"Yes! Yes!" came a muffled, panicked voice. "Thank God!"

"Whoa!" Jeremy said. "That sounds like Deion!" They moved to the car, and Jeremy put his ear to the trunk lid. "Deion?" he said, "Is that you?"

"Yes!" came the voice.

Jeremy looked at David in astonishment. "It's Deion!" he said, pointing to the trunk. "Deion's in there!" He leaned closer to the trunk lid again. "Deion! What the heck are you doing in there?"

"Get me out!" came the anguished reply.

They were momentarily puzzled as to how to accomplish that, and Deion kept crying out for help. At last Jeremy hurried around to the car's driver's side door. It wasn't locked, and after a few seconds of hunting around the controls, he found the trunk release and pressed it. The trunk lid sprang open and David took a step back.

There, folded up among some tools with his back wrapping awkwardly around the curve of a spare tire was Deion, blinking in the light. He looked a fright, disheveled and ragged with bits of grass and other detritus in his hair, his face smeared with sweat and his shirt with grease.

"Oh, thank God!" he said, gulping in the fresh air. "Thank God! I thought I would die in here."

They took hold of his arms to lift him, groaning as his limbs straightened from their confinement, out of the trunk. Jeremy struggled to untangle his legs from a set of jumper cables. They finally got him out and half-carried him over to lean on the hood of Jeremy's car.

"What the heck, Deion?" Jeremy asked again.

"That maniac!" Deion gasped, his voice raspy and hoarse. "That maniac put me in there!"

"Blaney?" said David.

Deion glared at him. "Any other maniacs we been running around with lately?"

"What happened?"

Deion groaned again. "I don't even know! We were going to take Laura…" Deion stopped and looked at David. "Lord," he said. "In the *baptistry*?" David looked away. "I didn't think she even *liked* you."

"I know, right?" said Jeremy.

"All right, all right! How did you end up in there?"

After a moment's panting, Deion continued. "We were going to take Laura home, and Blaney said we should come here first, get our own vehicles. That made sense, so we came this way. I was driving, and he was in the back seat with Laura. He had to practically sit on her, 'cause she kept trying to get out again, even while the car was moving. She was ranting and raving and yelling, 'Where's David? We have a bond!' Babbling all kinds of stuff about you and about Glenda, cussing me and Blaney, and going on about some 'man.' She wasn't making any sense, as far as I could tell. When she finally wound down a little, Blaney started asking her questions." Deion became more agitated, waving his arms. "They were talking low! Whispering! I couldn't hear! I told him that, but he wouldn't believe me!"

"What then?" said David.

"We got here and got out. I was going to take Laura in my car, leave her car here. That's when he pulled his gun."

"What?"

"He pulled his gun on me! *Again*! He said he wasn't gonna let me tip them off. Tip who off? About what? I didn't know what he was talking about! He wouldn't listen. He was crazy. I thought this time he was really gonna shoot me! But he just took my phone and keys and made me get in the trunk!" He leaned forward, head in his hands. "Oh my Lord! Mary! He just threw my stuff in the car, and I could hear the phone ringing. I know it was her looking for me. Rang and rang until I guess the battery died. Oh Lord!"

"What about Laura?" asked David. "What did he do with her?"

"I don't know!" Deion cried. "Didn't you hear me? I was in the trunk! All night long! I thought I was going to suffocate!"

"Why didn't you use the door latch?"

David and Deion looked at Jeremy. "Do what?" said Deion.

Jeremy jerked a thumb toward the car. "Why didn't you just open the trunk with the door latch?"

"What are you talking about?"

"The door latch!" Jeremy repeated, with a "duh" chuckle. "Every car made in like, the last twenty years has had a manual door latch inside the trunk." He stepped to Deion's car and pointed to a small, t-shaped handle inset into the trunk lid. "See?" Deion went very still and stared in silence for a long moment. Jeremy gripped the little handle. "See? All you gotta do is—"

"Shut up, Jeremy!" Deion shouted. "Will you for once just shut the hell up?" He leaned far forward, face in hands and began to weep.

"Sorry," Jeremy said. He jerked his head toward Deion and gave David a "what's with him?" look.

32

Deion showed no signs of calming down.

David, unable to think of anything else to do, put a hand on his shoulder, his intention being to say something consoling, though he wasn't sure what that would be. But when Deion felt David's touch, he leapt to his feet and stumbled away.

"Don't touch me!" he cried. He roughly wiped the tears from his eyes with the cuff of one sleeve and stood up straight. "Doesn't matter anyway!" he announced. "Because it's God's will. God put me in that trunk! So I could figure it out."

David said, "Figure what out?"

"All of it. *All* of it!" Deion swept an arm around in a wide arc as though indicating the entire Universe. "I had plenty of time. In there!" He jabbed a finger at the Nissan's trunk. "Time to think. About EVERYTHING! And I have. Figured. It. Out!"

"Come on, Deion," said David. "You should probably–"

"I don't even blame Blaney," Deion said, and gave a very unsettling laugh. His face had taken on a sort of ecstatic glow. David looked at Jeremy, realizing even as he did so that there would be little help forthcoming from that quarter. "He's a racist asshole, sure! But this?" He pointed, first at the ground in front of him, then, rapidly, at himself, David, Jeremy, and finally the sky. "This, what's going on? In this, he's just a... He ain't nothing but a..." He searched for a word, his face twisted with the effort.

"A what?" said Jeremy.

"That piece. The chess piece. The little one."

"Pawn?" David ventured.

"YES!" Deion shouted. Then, "No! Well, yes, kind of. That is what he is. Kind of. That's what we all is! Are! So it isn't his fault! And it isn't my fault, or Jeremy's fault. It isn't even Glenda's fault."

"Deion," said David. "Why don't we go inside? You're probably dehydrated."

Deion smiled slyly. He shook a finger at David. "And you! You were the key."

"*I* was the key?" David said. "To what?"

"To me figuring it all out! See? Because I started thinking about what I already thought before. How could David not know? How could anybody be that naïve, that...*clueless*? It just doesn't seem possible!" Deion began to pace back and forth on the lawn. He stumbled, looked down and found that he was standing in a rut, a trench Rolly Blaney's truck had dug there the day before. He looked up again. "I blamed her at first. 'The lips of the adulteress drip honey, but she is as bitter as wormwood!' Proverbs! Huh? Right? But no! It isn't her fault, either. Not really. It's her, but it isn't *her*! Laura, too! See?"

"Hey Deion," Jeremy said, "You're kinda freaking me out."

"That's why you couldn't see it! That's what I realized." Deion reached out toward David, clenched his fists. "When I was a drunk, David," he said, voice quivering, "When I was a useless, broken-down drunk. When I debased myself in every way. You know the one thing I never did?"

David felt himself weakening. He leaned on the fender of Jeremy's car. "Deion," he said, "please..."

"I never cheated on my wife! Not once!" He placed his left hand on his heart and raised his right, like a Boy Scout taking an oath. "Hand to God, not once! So why? Why did I do it now?"

"Deion, I don't want to hear about how–"

"There's only one explanation!" Deion cried. "Only one! I got to thinking, in there...in the dark! So...dark!" He choked back a sob, but went on. "I thought, could any woman, any *human* woman, marry David Burkitt, be so outwardly godly, but then want to seduce *me*? And him!" He pointed at Jeremy. "And Rolly Blaney? *Rolly Blaney*! Plus... God only knows who else?" David thought of Laura and turned away, but Deion lunged forward, pointing at him. "You were the key!" he said again, breathlessly. "Because I realized, David *couldn't* be that clueless! David *couldn't* be that stupid! Nobody could!"

"Thanks," said David.

He tried again to turn away, but Deion grabbed his arm, twisting him around. "And what you did last night? In the church! With *Laura*, of all people? That clenches it, David! It isn't your fault! None of this is our fault!" He leaned in close. David tried to pull away, but Deion had his arm in a painfully tight grip. When he spoke, the words came out in a harsh whisper.

"She's a demon, David."

David said nothing. Deion smiled and slowly nodded. Jeremy broke the silence. "What did he say?"

"I said, she's a demon!" Deion cried, "A succubus!"

"Whoa," said Jeremy, "You really think so?"

"Jeremy!" David said, "For God's sake! Deion, let go of me!"

"I saw it all at last!" Deion shook David's arm. "God showed me. We've been doing His work, right? All of us! And Satan didn't like it! So he sent his minion into Glenda and launched her at us like a torpedo! To infiltrate, to sow discord and to disrupt what we're doing! And it's been working! But now we're on to him!" He stepped back, smiling triumphantly.

"Would explain a lot," Jeremy said reasonably.

"Jeremy!"

"You're darn right it does!" Deion said. "And Blaney! Even *that* makes sense. He's being used, too, though he doesn't know it! Even though he's a vile, racist atheist, God is using him! Praise God!

Using him the same way He used the heathen rulers to chastise the wayward Children of Israel!"

"How do you figure?" asked Jeremy, warming to the theory.

"Blaney was onto something last night, though I don't know what it was. Laura told him something, and he has a part to play. I feel it! It came to me in there–" he pointed at the car's trunk. "In the darkness. God made it known to me! Blaney is His avenging angel!"

"What came to you in there," David said, "was oxygen deprivation. And maybe some fumes from the gas tank." All this time he'd been thinking he might be losing his mind. Now it seemed he might be the only one around who wasn't. "You need to lie down and get some rest!"

Deion shook a finger at him, his triumphant expression undimmed. "I'm going home, yes," he said. "I'm going home to tell Mary everything, and she will understand. We've been in the grip of nameless Evil. But the tide is turning! The tide is turning!"

With that, Deion bounded past Jeremy and got into his car. David and Jeremy watched as he started the engine and lurched ahead, narrowly missed the rear of David's car, made a tight semicircle and ripped across David's lawn, adding a new pair of ruts. He drove off the curb with a bang, the trunk bouncing open and disgorging a scattering of objects into the street before rebounding and slamming shut with a resounding boom. There was a screech of brakes as the car managed a left turn at the corner, and it was gone.

"Deion," said David at last, "has lost his mind."

"Are you sure?" said Jeremy.

David slumped against Jeremy's car. "Come on, Jeremy. Please."

Jeremy walked over to David, his demeanor serious. "It does fit the available evidence."

"Goodbye, Jeremy." David pushed himself with some difficulty off the car and started up the drive toward his front door, stepping gingerly on his bare feet.

"Sure, it sounds kinda crazy," Jeremy said, "but maybe that's part of it, see? Brother Dumond says the greatest trick the Devil ever pulled was convincing the world he doesn't exist."

David paused. "I'm pretty sure that was Kevin Spacey." He continued across the lawn.

"Jesus cast out demons," Jeremy went on, "That's right there in the Bible. And you know there are angels. If there are angels, then there must be demons. That's just common sense."

"If you say so," David said wearily. "I'm going inside now. Thanks again for the ride and...everything."

"What I don't get," Jeremy called after him, "is the part about what Rolly Blaney has to do with it. If there's a demon in Glenda, what's he supposed to do about it?"

"Goodbye, Jeremy," David repeated, waving a hand without looking back.

"Rolly Blaney," said Jeremy, "seems more like a 'shoot first, exorcize later' kind of guy." But David had reached his front door and did not hear him.

33

As soon as he closed the door behind himself, David had a staggeringly strong sense of deja vu. He realized that he was experiencing the exact feeling that he had...he couldn't believe that it was just yesterday. The feeling that, though the house was quiet, he was not alone. He glanced at the bookshelf and saw the empty space that usually held their engraved Bible. He saw the book lying on the coffee table where he had put it down yesterday before moving into the kitchen to discover...all the things he was to discover. The light was on in the kitchen now. Had it been left on last night? Could be. He didn't remember turning it off. But the television was off, and he was pretty sure that it had been left on.

He eased slowly and quietly across the room and looked warily around the edge of the doorway into the kitchen. Bitsy the cat sat on the floor mat in front of the sink, one hind leg thrust into the air, licking her crotch. She paused and looked at him, then, finding nothing in him to hold her interest, went back to what she was doing.

There were sounds. A rustle. A *clunk*. Someone was in there, just out of sight. He flashed back again to (seriously, was it just) the day before. Finding Rolly Blaney in his kitchen, bringing into his home, along with the stink of his cigarette, the open floodgates of all David's misery. *If he's here again,* David thought, *I'll kill myself.* David smelled something. But it wasn't cigarettes.

It was (*wake up and smell the*) coffee.

A flame of hope ignited in his brain. Was it possible? Could it be true?

He stepped around the corner and there she was. Glenda was at the stove in her fuzzy, blue bathrobe, just as he had seen her so many other mornings before the world fell off its axis and rolled into the gutter. She was back. Could it even be that she hadn't ever been gone at all? Maybe his world hadn't actually collapsed. Against all odds it actually *had* all been a nightmare. A wave rose up inside him–of joy this time, rather than despair. A loving God existed after all. David opened his mouth to utter a joyous exclamation.

But then he noticed some things.

He noticed, for instance, that Glenda seemed to be several inches shorter than usual; her robe almost dragged the floor. He noticed that Glenda's hair was now brick red. His brain fired all its synapses at once, struggling to conjure explanations for these discrepancies. Because it *was* Glenda. It *had to be* Glenda. As his brain spun out of control, she turned from the stove to face him, waving a spatula in tiny circles like a queen with her scepter.

"Morning, Sunshine," said Laura. "Scrambled or fried?"

34

A few miles away, the Thing, as Jeremy called it, or more officially the Rally to Keep Tennessee Safe for Christianity, was beginning to gear up. It was a nice day for it.

The evening before, a truck had parked its flatbed trailer in the open lot across Lakeview Road from the Boyd County Islamic Center. Early this morning, members of the maintenance and media teams from the Great Rock Church arrived to set up chairs on the trailer, along with a sound system and microphone. Cars began to appear and park in the lot behind the flatbed and up and down the shoulder on the north side of the road. People began milling around the lot in front of the flatbed. Promptly at 8:00 a.m. music blared from the speakers. The first selection: *Onward Christian Soldiers.*

As cars began to arrive on the north side of Lakeview Road, cars were also appearing on the south side, first into the parking lot of the Boyd County Islamic Center, then spilling onto the southern shoulders. As traffic began to take on county fair proportions, three cars from the Boyd County Sheriff's Department arrived, and deputies took to the pavement to try to get things under control, mainly through the use of stern looks and indecipherable hand signals. This took a traffic situation which had been busy but generally orderly and turned it into something resembling rush hour in Mumbai.

About this time vehicles with television station logos on the doors began to arrive. A remote truck from one of the Memphis stations pulled into a space near the flatbed and began to slowly crank its microwave antenna toward the deepening blue of the morning sky.

Signs began to pop up here and there on both sides of the road, bearing slogans of exclusivity on one side, inclusivity on the other. The signs on the north side of the road showed generally more emphatic sentiments, while those on the south side of the road tended to sport better spelling. It became quickly obvious that students and faculty of the college were turning out in large numbers to support their friends and colleagues. A bus arrived from First Baptist Church driven by Brother Birdsong. It began disgorging a stream of parishioners at the Islamic Center's gate, which further snarled traffic, since many of those parishioners moved rather slowly and a few required aluminum walkers. People on both sides of the road began to encroach on the pavement, a few shouting across the road in one direction or the other, all ignoring or unable to hear orders from the deputies to step back.

One of the sheriff's deputies ran to his car, got on his radio and requested more help, maybe from the Tennessee Highway Patrol. "This here," he told the dispatcher breathlessly, "is getting set to turn into a real clusterfuck!" He then apologized for his use of French over the radio.

All traffic had pretty much come to a halt by the time Jeremy arrived, and he was forced to park a good distance down the road. He jogged up the northern shoulder, struggling with his camera bag, extra heavy because he had brought extra batteries, toward the flatbed stage. He would be able to get a panoramic shot of the activities from up there before mingling with the crowd. Already mentally editing footage he had yet to shoot, he failed to notice what should have been a familiar vehicle parked on the shoulder, or to notice who should have been a familiar figure in the driver's seat.

That figure had not left the vehicle yet because Keeping Tennessee Safe for Christianity, though previously of great interest to him, had ceased to matter to him at all now. He was here for a different purpose entirely, a very specific purpose, and it did not involve any of the people in this crowd, north side of the road nor south. Not yet anyway. His reasons for being here were intensely personal. He had been made a fool of. And nobody, man or woman, Christian or heathen, was going to make a fool of him and get away with it.

He popped the clip from his pistol and checked that it was full, which he already knew it was. It was only a backup anyway. The real firepower was under a blanket in the back seat.

About this time there came from behind him the roar of an engine and a chorus of blaring car horns. He checked the side mirror on the passenger side. A large pickup truck was approaching, bullying its way directly up the center of the road, intimidating cars on either side out of its way. The truck was painted in a jungle camouflage motif, and the bed appeared to be filled with men dressed to match the truck.

A stroke of luck. This would make for perfect cover. He cinched up a strap on his tactical vest and opened his door.

35

With no energy left with which to resist the ineluctable and inscrutable Forces of Chaos and Madness which had enveloped him, David opted for scrambled.

"Scrambled it is," said Laura.

David lowered himself slowly into one of the chairs at the table, carefully so as to avoid missing it and falling onto the floor. He found that he had now been shocked so often that shock was actually getting a little boring. He really had to stop falling for that "only a dream" thing his brain kept setting in front of him and then snatching away like Lucy with her football.

Laura began cracking eggs, one in each hand, expertly into a frying pan before her. When she had cracked what she considered to be enough, she pivoted to the trash can next to the counter and threw in the shells. She opened a cabinet above the counter and plucked out a coffee cup, while the other hand yanked the urn from the coffeemaker on the counter. With another pirouette she set the cup in front of David and poured it full. She smirked at his expression. "I used to be a waitress," she said. She turned away and put the coffee pot back in the coffee maker. "Among other things." She stepped back to the stove, grabbed up her spatula and began stirring the eggs in the pan.

David watched her back. He had never really given Laura a lot of thought, other than to wonder idly why she seemed to be in such a bad mood all the time. To be honest, he had generally tried to avoid her. That she should suddenly be so deeply and bizarrely embedded in his life added even more to his feeling of unreality. As though feeling his gaze, she glanced over her shoulder, gave a chuckle at whatever his expression was now, and turned away again. David tried to think of something to say. Or rather, he tried to decide among the various options. What was she doing here? Why was she wearing his wife's robe? Or should he go ahead and address the terrible, terrible specter of the night before? That last option, the weightiest by far, was the one he dreaded most. Laura let him avoid the decision by speaking first.

"You 'boys' get everything worked out?"

"Boys?" David picked up the coffee cup. The sarcastic edge he was used to hearing in her voice seemed to be back, at least for the moment. It made him nervous, but he preferred it to the alternative.

"I saw you out there. With Frick and Frack. I'm glad you didn't bring them in here." She muttered something unintelligible under her breath.

Me, too, David thought. "Have you... Have you been here all night?"

"Since Rolly Blaney dumped me and stole my car, yeah," she said. "I fell asleep on your sofa." She turned to face him. "I hope you don't mind me using *her* robe. My dress was a little...mussed, so I sponged it off and hung it up." she smiled slyly. "And..." With a sudden move she snatched the robe open.

David jerked, sloshing coffee onto the table. To his indescribable relief, beneath the robe she was wearing gray sweatpants and a sweatshirt with his old college's logo. She laughed. "...I borrowed some of your stuff. I hope that's all right, too."

"Yes, yes," David said, putting the coffee carefully down, "fine, no problem." Laura cinched the robe closed again and turned back to the eggs. "Laura... About last night..."

"I know!" Laura said, shaking her head. "Wow! That was terribly naughty of us, wasn't it? But in our defense," she looked over her shoulder. "We were drunk." She picked up the pan and began scraping the eggs onto a plate.

"That isn't so much a defense," said David, "as a separate offense."

"I'm guessing you don't usually drink much. Or at all?" She turned off the stove burner, did another economical waitress pivot, and set the plate down in front of him. "I do, but not usually *that* much. But we'd both had a rough day, hadn't we?" She pulled a fork from the pocket of her robe and set it next to the plate. She pulled out the chair across from him and sat down.

David looked at the eggs, avoiding her eyes. "Thank you," he said.

She produced, seemingly out of nowhere, salt and pepper shakers in the shape of two Coca-Cola bottles and slid them across the table to him. "You're welcome."

David sighed. "Laura," he said. She leaned on one elbow and set her chin in her hand. "I..." She raised her eyebrows expectantly. "I... I thought you didn't even like me."

"Who says I do now?" He said nothing and after an uncomfortable moment she giggled. "I was jealous, I guess. Of what you had, and how you didn't have to hide it. But hey!" She leaned back in her chair and thrust her hands into the robe's pockets. "Turns out neither of us really had much of anything, did we? At last the scales have fallen from our eyes."

"Like Paul," David muttered automatically, thinking, however, that he was unaware of anything having fallen from his own eyes. If anything, things were blurrier now than they had ever been.

"Paul who?" said Laura.

To avoid replying to that, David ate a mouthful of eggs. He realized that he was ravenous. He reached for the saltshaker.

Laura watched him eat with a bemused expression. "Deion sure tore out of here," she said at last.

David nodded. "He was pretty traumatized," he said around the eggs. "He was locked in the trunk of his car most of the night."

Laura laughed. "I know!"

David stopped chewing and looked at her. "You knew he was in there?"

"Sure. I was there when Blaney put him in, wasn't I?"

"Why didn't you let him out?"

"Why didn't he let *himself* out? Every car trunk has one of those little pull-handles. Doesn't surprise me, though. He couldn't find his ass with both hands. His wife runs that TV station." David's expression seemed to annoy her. "What do I care if he's locked in a trunk? If I had my way I'd put 'em all in a trunk, then drive the car into the river!" She scowled and wriggled in her chair.

David found the sudden swings in her mood more than a bit disconcerting. "Deion," he said, "went a little batty in there. He even seems to think that Glenda...and you, too, I guess...might be temptresses sent by Satan."

Laura laughed louder this time. "That's great! The booze lets *you* off the hook, and the Devil made *him* do it. I thought you people believed in Free Will."

David didn't know what to make of that "you people." Since she worked for a religious broadcasting organization, he had assumed she was a devoted Christian herself, in spite of showing few signs of interest in Christian fellowship. Now he wondered how she had ever come to work for Channel 38 in the first place.

"I wonder if his wife will buy that story?" she said. "Knowing her, she might." A twinkle seemed to come back into her eyes. "What about you? Think it was just the booze, or did I *bewitch* you last night?"

Looking at her gleaming, mocking eyes, had David been a Catholic he would have crossed himself. Instead, he shook his head, sorry he had mentioned it. "So," he said, turning his attention back to the eggs, "Blaney took your car. Have you called the police?"

Laura's eyes narrowed. She looked around the room. "All this Coke stuff is a bit much, isn't it? I knew she was into collecting it, but..." She noticed Bitsy, now sitting next to her bowl in the standard pose she assumed in hopes of fooling the person who hadn't just fed her into thinking she hadn't just been fed by the person who had. "I fed your cat. He seemed hungry. What's his name?"

"It's a her," said David. "Bitsy." He almost made some comment about cats and vague genders, but it died on his tongue. "It's Glenda's cat, really. She doesn't like me much." To his annoyance, Laura seemed to find this amusing. Also, her awkward change of subject from Blaney to cat following so closely on his own awkward change of subject from temptresses to Blaney made David curious. "It sounds like Blaney has gone completely off the rails, though with him that may be a subtle difference. And he did steal your car. Maybe we should report it to–"

"I'll get my car back eventually," she said. "And Blaney's all right wherever he is. How are the eggs?"

"Very good. Thank you again."

"Don't mention it," she said.

She certainly didn't seem to want to talk about Blaney. David said, "Deion said you told Blaney something last night."

"I told everybody a lot of things. Where they could go, how they should burn when they got there. I guess I gave an earful to all and sundry. Where did you go, by the way? I sat up thinking you'd come home. I thought you might want to finish what we started."

The last bite of egg stuck momentarily in David's throat, and he forced it down with some difficulty. "Last night," he said, "before you... Before we..."

Laura smiled. "Before we what?"

"You said *him*. You said Glenda had left me...us...for *him*. Did you tell Blaney that, too? Who were you talking about?"

Laura's smile withered. She got up and turned away. Seeking a reason to have done so, she snatched up the egg carton and returned it to the refrigerator. "Like I said, I was drunk! Blaney was too, or maybe he was on something else. He acted like it, waving that gun around."

"Who were you talking about, Laura?" he insisted. "Who's 'him?'"

"Nobody," she said, and shrugged. "Just... *Him*. Whoever he is. I mean, assuming it *is* a him."

David reddened. *So many shocks...* But he wouldn't let himself be distracted. "You know who Glenda is with, don't you? How do you know?"

"I hear things, that's all," she said, and leaned on the counter. "Why don't you stop asking questions and enjoy your breakfast? Then you can take a nice shower. In fact, if you want, we could both–"

"Stop it, Laura!" David put his fork down.

They sat and stood in silence for a long moment. "Right," Laura said at last. "I get it. She doesn't want me, and sober you don't want me, either. I saw it in your eyes before." She plucked at the lapels of her robe. "If I'd had nothing on under this, you'd have run out of the house, wouldn't you?"

David couldn't hold her gaze. "Last night should never have happened. I mean, where we were..." He cringed once again at the memory. "That was extra wrong. But it would have been wrong anywhere. It just was. For one thing, I'm still a married man." He sounded prim and silly to himself as he said it.

Laura barked a bitter laugh. "You may think so, but she sure as shit doesn't! She's moved on, trust me! From both of us." Muscles twitched in her jaw. Her voice became icy and her next statement was an eerie echo from the day before. "And if she was gonna leave you for anybody, it was supposed to be *me*!"

"Moved on where?" he demanded. "Who with? And how do you know this?" Laura did not answer. "You told Blaney, didn't you? That's the part I don't understand. And Blaney thought Deion heard you, so he locked him up. He thought Deion would...what? Tip somebody off? Who? About what?" Laura said nothing. "Blaney is a crazy man! Why would you tell him, but you won't tell me?"

Laura's expression hardened into a threatening scowl. David opened his mouth to say more, but before he could, she lunged toward him, fists clenched and pressed to her sides, a movement so abrupt that it sent Bitsy scurrying into the safety of the laundry room.

"I told him *because* he's crazy!"

"What do you–"

"Why would I tell *you*?" she snarled. "What good would that do? If I told you, I know exactly what you'd do, Mr. Goody-Two-Shoes! Nothing. No! Worse than nothing!" Her voice filled with contempt. "You'd probably *forgive* them!"

David said, "But Blaney...?"

"Blaney," Laura said with a chilling smile, "will *kill* them."

36

"A right unexercised," shouted the heavily armed man, "is no right at all."

He was speaking to a petite, blond, professionally coiffed woman almost a foot shorter than himself who was holding a microphone near his chin. A woman with a much less expensive hairstyle at the tiny woman's shoulder pointed a video camera at him. The man was dressed in a hodgepodge of military and pseudo-military paraphernalia topped by a camouflage boonie hat. He stood with one hand on the butt of a rifle swinging on a lanyard clipped to his bullet-proof vest.

"But what has that got to do with—" the woman with the microphone shouted back.

"Do what?" said the man.

"With this protest!" the tiny woman screamed.

They were shouting at one another over the dreadful cacophony raging all around them. The nearby loudspeakers on the flatbed trailer were once more blaring *Onward Christian Soldiers*, and people around them who knew the words, as well as many more who didn't, were singing along. At the same time, the crowd on the opposite side of Lakeview Road had gotten their own sound system set up and were blasting out *Give Peace A Chance*, to which everyone knew the words. There were other random shouts and chants, plus the non-stop honking of horns from the cars of curious passersby as well as motorists who had simply made a tragically unlucky choice of route, all now creeping along the road through the middle of the confrontation. To top it all off, there were the piercing stabs of sirens of the Tennessee Highway Patrol, several of whose officers had recently arrived and were in the process of getting things under control by completely blocking traffic at either end of the activities.

The man in the military garb, Josh Waley, represented, as he was happy to explain at length, a group called Tennessee Free-to-Carry, an organization that advocated the broadest possible interpretation of the 2nd Amendment to the U.S. Constitution, and which demonstrated this advocacy by showing up at various public events–demonstrations, campaign events, supermarket openings–armed to the teeth, as he was now, and as were the five–or as of a few minutes ago, six–compatriots gathered around and behind him. He launched into his mostly inaudible prepared explanation of the group's goals and methods, and the television reporter who had incorrectly assumed that a man dressed so outrageously must have something interesting to say gave a meaningful look to her camera operator, who surreptitiously stopped recording. She kept nodding attentively until the man seemed to pause, at which point she shouted, "Thanks!" and scurried away, camera following close behind, to cross the road and talk to someone on the other side who was hopefully at least tangentially connected to the event at hand.

A small, harried-looking man sporting a graying combover, a checked jacket, and a tie with a gold, embroidered cross took this opportunity to approach. "Sir! Sir!" he shouted. "Can I ask a favor?" This was Maurice Thurlow, one of the deacons, or as Reverend Dumond referred to them, "assistants" from the Great Rock Church. His was the thankless job of trying to keep the festivities in sync with the pre-arranged program, an endeavor pretty much doomed from the outset. Even the National Anthem, which was supposed to start the event, wasn't going to go off as scheduled because the woman who was slated to sing it hadn't arrived yet. He now proceeded to shout into the armed man's ear that, while he wholeheartedly concurred with Tennessee Free-to-Carry's agenda, knew that Reverend

Dumond did, and was certain Jesus did as well, the organizers would greatly appreciate it if he and his companions could move away from directly in front of the stage, as they were interfering with gathering an audience there by scaring the shit out of everybody.

With the sort of dark expression one never wishes to see on the face of a man holding an automatic weapon, the leader of the Tennessee Free-to-Carry group reluctantly assented and began gathering his group and directing them farther over to one side of the flatbed, away from the prime real estate at the feet of the upcoming speakers.

Jeremy, who was on the flatbed near the folding chairs, caught this small drama with his own video camera before panning over to look at the various organizers and dignitaries awaiting the official beginning of the rally. He recognized the State Legislator who had introduced the Guaranteeing Religious Freedom Bill, which should when passed guarantee the freedom of certain specific religions in the state of Tennessee to the exclusion of certain...well, all, really...others. There were also some more church deacons and a car dealer locally famous for his amusing television commercials. Reverend Dumond had yet to arrive, the general consensus being that he was either waiting to make a dramatic entrance or was hopelessly trapped in traffic, or both.

Jeremy turned to get another wide shot and noticed as he panned across the roiling vista before him that the crowd on the far side of Lakeview Road was definitely swelling at a rate greater than that on his own. They seemed to have a better sound system, too, he noted with some chagrin.

Maurice Thurlow came thumping up the steps onto the stage, shouting, "O.K.! O.K.! Will do!" into a walkie-talkie, which he was using instead of a cell phone for some reason. He stepped to the microphone, frantically waving at the young man at the sound board. After making violent cutting gestures near his throat with one hand and thumping energetically on the microphone with the other, he managed to get his message across. The music cut out and was replaced by the thumping, followed by a momentary screech of feedback. Then Thurlow spoke.

"Ladies and Gentlemen," he said, the words echoing and reverberating. A chorus of boo's erupted from the crowd across the road. "Ladies and Gentlemen! My fellow *Christians*!" A less impressive roar of approval from the north side of the road. The vibe struck Jeremy like that of opposing bleachers at a football game, and it was starting to sound like the Muslims were the home team. "I'd like to introduce to you now one of our greatest supporters in the statehouse in Nashville! A true patriot and a true Christian..."

At his name the politician stepped up to the microphone to a smattering of applause barely audible over the music from across the road, which was now *All You Need Is Love*. Clearly a John Lennon fan was in charge of the playlist over there. Jeremy wasn't particularly interested in what the politician had to say, but felt that an over-the-shoulder shot was called for. He was thwarted in this when Maurice Thurlow's nose appeared enormous in his viewfinder. There followed a short, sharp pissing match which Jeremy quickly lost, despite pointing out the Channel 38 t-shirt he was now wearing. Deacon Thurlow insisted that the guy from the media department of the Great Rock Church was in charge of recording the event. Jeremy had seen that camera guy standing around near his car, bored, obviously waiting for Reverend Dumond to appear on the scene, his many-pocketed photographer's vest, bulky tripod and large, expensive, 10 bit/8K camera causing Jeremy to shatter the 10th Commandment.

The state legislator, distracted, gave them both a dirty look, and a moment later Jeremy found himself shoved onto the steps at the edge of the flatbed. Once again, Philistines had deprived the world of what would have been a great shot.

Jeremy felt a tug at his shirt and turned to find Mary Mullins standing at his side. She was wearing a long, flowery dress fancier than any he had seen her wear at the station, and dangling gold earrings. She also wore a decidedly troubled expression.

"Oh! Hey, Mary! Didn't know you were here! Nice earrings!"

Mary gestured for him to follow her and moved over to a space behind the loudspeakers where it was easier to carry on a conversation. "Have you heard from Deion?" she said.

"Oh wow," Jeremy said, "haven't you seen him? He said he was going to find you."

"When?" She clutched at his arm and put a hand on her chest as though she might swoon. "When did you see him? I've been scared to death! Is he all right?"

"Yeah," said Jeremy, "he's O.K. Well, pretty much O.K. He would have been in touch, but he was locked in the trunk all night."

"What?"

"Rolly Blaney locked him in the trunk of his car. Deion's car, I mean. And– Funny story! Deion apparently didn't know that every car in the last twenty years–"

"Locked him in the trunk!" Mary cried. "What on Earth are you talking about?"

"Uh..." Jeremy hesitated. "It's kind of a long story. You better hear it from him. He'll probably call you as soon as he gets a chance to charge his phone."

"Oh my Lord! Jeremy! You know Deion is diabetic. When his blood sugar gets off, he can have one of his spells!"

Jeremy gaped at her, then to her amazement, laughed. "Ooooh! His blood sugar! Right! That explains it! Deion said it was God, and Dave said it was gas fumes, but blood sugar makes even more sense! Kind of a relief, really, because he said–"

"Oh, for the love of–" Mary turned and hurried away, muttering something about idiots. Jeremy followed, pausing at the top of the steps.

He noticed–they were hard to miss–the Free-to-Carry group all huddled up a few yards away, presumably conferring over the best way to get back into the limelight. All huddled up, that is, except for one member who stood apart, his back to the rest of the group, scanning the crowd in the direction of the road. There was something about that man that Jeremy found familiar. He raised his camera to his eye and zoomed in to its greatest extent. After a moment the man turned in his direction and Jeremy immediately recognized the glowering, angry face in spite of his pulled-low cap and mirrored sunglasses.

"Hey," he said to no one in particular. "Speak of the Devil."

37

"Our basic message is pretty simple," said Brother Birdsong to the small television reporter. "Support your neighbors. After all, the faith of the folks here at the Center may be different from mine, but we still share the same basic values–the values everybody shares, or *should* share. I think–and you can see from this crowd that many folks around here seem to agree–that it's better to celebrate our similarities than to exaggerate and prey upon our differences."

The reporter nodded enthusiastically, not so much in agreement as in satisfaction at finally getting a usable soundbite from *somebody*. She stuck her microphone near her own mouth and said, "Speaking of preying on differences, what would you have to say to Raymond Dumond, who has organized the protest?"

"I've spoken to Reverend Dumond. He knows my feelings. I don't need to talk to him through the TV."

"He seemed to be talking to you, or people like you, on TV last night," she said.

"I didn't catch that program," said Brother Birdsong. "Be sure to talk to Dr. Bahri," he went on, pointing to a table set up near the front door of the Islamic Center. "He's over there by the refreshments." Nodding, the pair began moving in that direction. "And try that Turkish baklava Mrs. Baykara made! It's delicious!"

"I thought baklava was Greek," said the camera operator.

"Don't say that in front of Mrs. Baykara!" Brother Birdsong laughed. "Thank you!" With a wave they moved away. Mrs. Birdsong stepped up beside him. "Wonderful turnout!" she said, leaning in and speaking loudly.

"Better even than I hoped for," Brother Birdsong agreed. A voice, difficult to understand through the reverberations and the background roar of crowd and music, echoed from across the road and was answered by a growl from the people gathered along the near side. "I'm proud of our community for stepping up. But I'm a little worried by the tone of some of them. I'm going to step out there and try to remind everybody why we're here."

"You'll need a bullhorn!" said Mrs. Birdsong.

"What?" Brother Birdsong cupped a hand behind one ear. Mrs. Birdsong pointed at her own ear. "Ask Bryon to turn it down!" he shouted. She nodded and moved away.

Brother Birdsong made his way through the crowd, many of whom shook his hand or patted his back. The gathering within the Center's gates had taken on the air of a block party, with the attendees mostly oblivious to the group across the road whom they were ostensibly counter-protesting. This was not true, however, of those outside the gates along the roadside.

He saw that traffic had stopped now that the Highway Patrol had closed off the road, and the two groups faced each other across pavement empty except for a scattering of nervous sheriff's deputies and a couple of state police. Even this subset of the supporters of the Center seemed to outnumber the protesters who took to the roadside. Those seemed to be trying to make up for that fact by being individually louder and more aggressive. They shouted and shook their signs, their backs turned to the loquacious politician on the flatbed to whom no one seemed to be paying much attention. In ones and twos they stepped out into the road, yelling and shaking their fists, retreating reluctantly when the deputies approached and ordered them back. Looking down the line he saw that a few of his own people were similarly stepping into the road, taunting the other side.

Brother Birdsong stepped out into the road himself. He nodded and held up a "just give me a minute" finger to one of the deputies, who nodded indulgently back. Brother Birdsong faced his own group. The music blaring from the speakers in front of the Islamic Center hadn't gotten any quieter, so he tried to convey his message with smiles and calming gestures. Spontaneous applause broke out, and the mood seemed to lighten somewhat. The music had by this point segued into an acoustic guitar song that Brother Birdsong recognized but couldn't immediately place. A young woman with a flapper's bob of bright pink hair, dressed in shorts and a tie-dyed t-shirt–presumably one of the college students, he thought–came bouncing out of the crowd and grabbed his hands. She began to lead him in a twirling dance in the middle of the road, which brought a roar of approval from the south-side crowd and a phalanx of cell phone cameras pointed their way.

"Whoa, girl!" Brother Birdsong laughed, "I'm a Baptist! We don't dance!"

"You do today!" she said and twirled him around again.

The song, *Peace Train* by Steven Geogiu, better known as Cat Stevens, but who later changed that to Yusuf Islam, continued to play, and the two continued to twirl, as a black SUV with darkened windows was waved past the police car blocking the eastern approach and moved slowly up the road. On the flatbed Maurice Thurlow began to pry the microphone away from the Tennessee state legislator in order to announce the arrival of the star of the show.

38

The human mind is an amazing and mysterious thing.

Scientists, who have successfully explained so many complicated things, seem to bump into a wall when attempting to explain this thing they use to figure out all the other things. It's such a hard problem, in fact, that it is commonly known as The Hard Problem. How does one, after all, explain how a few pounds of meat can give rise to something capable of so many astonishing feats, not the least of which being the ability to be so self-aware as to ask the question of how that self-same few pounds of meat can do all those things? This difficulty is one reason that the explanation, "It's that way because God made it that way," is so appealing to so many people.

One of the mind's capabilities is its ability to run an immensely complex set of what one might call "background calculations" in an almost imperceptibly small fragment of time, then to spit a solution from what appears to the conscious mind to be out of nowhere. Consider, for example, the complexity of calculating the angles and forces needed to send a hollow sphere 9.5 inches in diameter and weighing 1.32 pounds a distance of 15 feet in a parabola such that it passes cleanly through a metal hoop 18 inches in diameter resting 10 feet off the ground. Yet the minds of many NBA players, most of which contain only a basic knowledge of Newtonian physics and at best a rudimentary grasp of calculus, on a regular basis successfully run these calculations and even actuate the forces necessary to perform the action. They run these calculations, furthermore, nearly instantaneously, and almost completely unconsciously. In fact, if the player consciously thinks about it too much, he will very likely get in his mind's way and miss his free throw.

When Laura spoke the words, *you'd forgive them* and *Blaney will kill them,* David's mind, there in his brain, in his skull, in his kitchen, went into a blinding burst of activity. In spite of all the shocks, psychological and chemical, it had been put through in the last few hours, his brain now managed to fire off a veritable storm of insightful cogitation and calculation. There was no logical sequence to these flashes; they went off almost simultaneously. But they somehow, some might say "miraculously," added up to comprehension that his addled conscious mind might not have been able to work out in a week of contemplation. Certain words and phrases came alive with associations and connections to previous knowledge and opinion, which then brought into existence insights, realizations, and, finally, impulses. And all of it took place in almost literally the blink of an eye.

There was the word *forgive.* It brought to David's mind those red words in his King James Bible, in which forgiveness was a major theme. Jesus even forgave the people who were crucifying him. (Luke. Some pretty Good Stuff in Luke.) The Apostle Paul and others tended to go on and on about *atonement,* that is, the necessity of doing penance or making amends for wrongdoing. Jesus, on the other hand, simply *forgave.* That was one reason David frankly liked Jesus better than Paul–Paul, with his stream of preachy letters telling people all around the Mediterranean to do this and do that, or else. David's mind now considered how, somewhat surprisingly given the literally inconceivable, to him anyway, level of betrayal involved, he had so far felt practically no animosity toward Glenda. He had wanted to find her, but not in order to chastise her. He just desperately wanted to understand what had happened, how it was possible, and whether it could somehow be rectified. So yes, his mind decided, no matter what she had done or with whom, he would forgive Glenda. He *did* forgive her. He had to. He loved her. Besides, vengeance was very Old Testament.

Which brought up the next words his mind latched onto: *Blaney will kill them.* Was Laura actually saying that Rolly Blaney would actually, literally do something so insane? He had to admit that nothing he had seen in his brief acquaintance with Blaney would seem to rule out the possibility. Laura's face, triumphant, there before his eyes as his mind did all this firing, left him no doubt that she at least believed it, and seemed to like the idea!

(At that instant and as a side effect of the thought of the psycho Rolly Blaney with his massive ego and Old Testament motivations, another unconscious part of David's brain sent an urgent, firebell message to his adrenal glands.)

Lastly there was the *them.* She said, kill *them.* There was that recurring burning question: Who was the other half of that *them?* And then his mind made the sharpest connection and most intuitive leap of all. It called up the words Laura had said earlier when asked how she knew what she knew: *I hear things.* With that, in the concluding milliseconds of the second that he stared at Laura's triumphant face, his mind ran through a myriad of possibilities and discarded them one by one until only one was left and the whole thing fell into place. Who *them* had to mean, where *they* almost certainly were, and what might be about to happen.

Also in that instant the adrenalin his brain had just called for was dumped into his bloodstream.

"You!" David screamed.

Laura recoiled so abruptly that she lost her balance and staggered back against the counter. Her feet shot out from under her, and she plopped down onto her behind. David rose from his chair, grabbed the table and hurled it to one side, where it slammed into the wall. His plate and coffee cup went flying, and a rain of Coca-Cola-themed doodads clattered down from the shelf above. He stepped toward her, pointing a finger much like the prophet Jeremiah probably did as he cried, "Hear ye the Word of the Lord, oh house of Jacob!"

"You," David shouted, "are a *receptionist*!" With that he turned and ran out of the room.

After a stunned moment, Laura said, "Administrative assistant!" Then she began to cry.

39

After he spotted Blaney, Jeremy hiked his camera bag higher on his shoulder and made his way toward him. He was curious about Blaney's motive for locking Deion in the trunk of his car and thought, naively, that Blaney might enlighten him on the subject. He also thought, even more naively, that Blaney might like to know that Deion, in spite of his lamentable ignorance of mandatory automotive safety devices, did eventually escape the trunk of his car. He was glad to have heard from Mary a secular explanation for Deion's supposedly divine revelations. The concept of Rolly Blaney as an instrument of God's Wrath had puzzled him in the extreme. Admittedly, wrath was one of Blaney's defining attributes, but he couldn't work out how God would have come into the picture.

"Hi, Mr. Blaney!" he said, speaking loudly over the din. Blaney did not react. He just continued to watch the road a few yards away. "It's me," Jeremy continued. "Jeremy? From last night?"

"Fuck off," said Blaney.

"Wow," Jeremy said. "That's pretty rude. I just thought you might like to know that—"

"Hey!" a voice called out, and a hand poked Jeremy's shoulder. It was Josh Waley, the heavily armed man Jeremy had seen talking to the reporter earlier. "You with a TV station?" he asked.

"Yeah," said Jeremy. "Channel 38. I'm the Chief Engineer."

"Engineer?" said Waley. He seemed to have difficulty slotting Jeremy into that job title. "But you got a camera, right?" He pointed at the one Jeremy held in his hand.

"Sure."

"Great! You want to do an interview?"

Jeremy looked around. There was no one else nearby except the other armed men. The crowd seemed to be giving them a wide berth. "With who?"

"Me! I'm Josh Waley, and I represent Tennessee Free-to-Carry. Our mission is to promote the freedom to–"

Blaney rounded on them. "Will both of you fuck off?" he snarled, and turned once again to his vigilant watch over the roadside.

"Whoa there, hoss!" said Waley. "Who you think you're talking to?"

"You, dipshit!" Blaney tossed over his shoulder.

Blaney seemed to be even more wrathful than usual this morning. Jeremy began to back away. "Hey guys," he said. "Let's be cool, OK?"

"Hey! Who the hell are you, anyway?" Waley demanded, taking a step toward Blaney. "You ain't even a member of the organization."

Blaney spun around and stepped up nose to nose with the man. "I wouldn't join your candy-ass 'organization' if you was handing out blowjobs and ice cream cones. Bunch of limp-dick wannabe commandos, dressed up like Halloween and marching around scaring limp-dick Liberals! I said *fuck off*!" Blaney returned to watching the road, having had his say.

Free-to-Carry Waley was stunned into silence. One of his compatriots standing nearby said dangerously, "*What* did he just say?"

Jeremy's first impulse was to hustle away as far as possible from what he feared might be a rapidly escalating situation, but his innate cameraman instincts made him raise his camera instead. As he was doing so, a black SUV with tinted windows was drawing up at the side of the road nearby. The drone of the Tennessee legislator was replaced by the breathless tones of Maurice Thurlow.

"Ladies and gentlemen," came Thurlow's voice through another short burst of feedback, "I am happy to announce the arrival of the man who has called us all here today..."

Blaney straightened and peered around the people blocking his view as the SUV came to a halt. He began to move forward. At that moment a hand fell on his shoulder. "Hey, smartass!" It was the compatriot of Free-to-Carry Waley, who had taken extreme offense at Blaney's characterization of himself and his compatriots as 'limp-dick wannabe commandos dressed up for Halloween.' "How would you like a—" he began.

He did not get to finish his offer of whatever it was he was about to offer–an ass-kicking of some sort, one assumes–because Blaney jerked to one side, swiveled, and rammed the butt of the rifle he was carrying into the man's nose. The man's head jerked back, sending an inverted catenary curve of blood arcing through the air as he flopped over backwards into a heavily armed and armored heap on the ground.

Blaney, acting once more as though that should have ended the matter, continued toward the road and the SUV, the back door of which had just swung open. A foot in an extremely expensive, probably Italian, shoe emerged and stepped onto the ground. Blaney worked the bolt on his rifle. He had taken about three steps when two men jumped onto his back.

The crowd clustered around the SUV burst into applause as Reverend Raymond Dumond, smile flashing, emerged from the vehicle. He was wearing a sportcoat today, but no tie, the top two or three buttons of his shirt open, showing his chest hair and his solidarity with the common man. He gave a friendly wave to all, turned and extended a hand to someone else in the back seat of the SUV.

Before that person could be handed out, everyone froze, listening.

A horrible, high-pitched, metallic screeching had swelled to fill the air, and was growing louder and louder. Reverend Dumond and all the people around the SUV turned and looked down Lakeview Road. A cloud of blue-black smoke was visible beyond the Highway Patrol car blocking the road, and at the front of that car a trooper was frantically waving at something approaching from that direction, ordering whatever it was to stop. As the crowd looked on in amazement, the trooper stopped waving, crouched for a moment, scooted a few steps one way then the other like a confused squirrel, and launched himself onto the hood of his car.

Around the car, very narrowly missing it and blasting through the space the trooper had occupied a moment before, there appeared a very old, light blue pickup truck trailing a spectacular, billowing plume of smoke. The roaring scream of its engine now became ear-splitting.

It was David Burkitt driving Rolly Blaney's truck at sixty miles per hour in second gear.

40

A few minutes prior to hurtling down Lakeview Road, and a few seconds after leaving Laura on her rump in his kitchen, David Burkitt hurtled out his front door, off his porch and into his front yard. He was in the throes of the rush from adrenalin and from all the realizations he had just had and continued to have.

The latest and current realization was the one that for the last twenty-four hours he had been a thing without agency–a leaf in a rushing stream, a ball in a pachinko game. He had been shoved this way and bounced that by forces beyond his control or comprehension through an impenetrable fog of confusion and shock. And the worst thing was, he had accepted it. He had simply acquiesced to the forces slapping him hither and thither. *I thought you people believed in Free Will?* Laura had a point. Now that he knew–he just *knew*–where Glenda had gone, who she had gone with, where they likely were, and what might possibly happen there, David made the determination to stop floating and to exercise his Free Will.

Enlightenment had come when his mind, with no help from David himself, put together Laura's words–*I hear things*–with the fact that in her capacity at the television station she had all the buttons for all the incoming and outgoing telephone lines under her fingertips at all times. He knew then what must have happened as certainly as if he had been standing at the reception desk when it took place. It must have happened yesterday (*only yesterday?*) morning, the morning Glenda disappeared. Laura was already acting strangely when he arrived for the meeting that afternoon, which meant Laura had *heard things* prior to that. What she had heard, he was certain, was Glenda on the phone with *him*. This meant *him* was at the television station yesterday. *Him* could not have been Deion or Jeremy, since they didn't know where Glenda was or, at that point, even that she had disappeared. It had to be someone else, and there was only one other someone else it could have been. When this all came to him, many things began at last to make sense.

Well, not *make sense* exactly, but at least to follow some sort of quasi-logical sequence.

David grabbed the handle of his car door but did not pull on it. He released it again and frantically slapped all his pockets. He had lost his keys. *What about Glenda's car?* He had no idea where her car key was, and the garage was blocked by his own car anyway. *What about a taxi?* He didn't have his phone. More importantly, the town didn't have a taxi service. He began to panic. Here he finally knew where he needed to go, and he had no way to get there.

I'll run. It's only three or four miles. He looked down. He was not wearing shoes. There was also the fact that he hadn't run more than about a hundred feet at a stretch since he was in high school.

David looked at the sky. He wondered again, wildly, just what he had done to rate this kind of treatment. From the moment Rolly Blaney– David gasped.

He began to run, not down the street, but around the corner of the garage. He continued around the side to the rear of the garage, hoping against hope, and found that he had not (*Keep Calm and Trust Jesus*) been entirely abandoned after all. Blaney's truck was there. He clambered into the seat, wrenched the door closed with a creak and a crunch, and reached for the ignition key.

The key was not there.

"All right!" he said aloud. "All right! Stay calm!" Things had gone his way once. It could happen again. He looked around the cab. Nothing on the seat, nothing on the dashboard. He leaned over and punched the push button of the glove compartment. The door flopped open, and he jammed a hand inside, raking the contents out into the floorboard. Cigarettes. An actual pair of gloves (the first he'd ever seen in a glove compartment). Papers, gum wrappers. A glass tube of some kind, scorched on one end.

No keys.

He gripped the steering wheel. How many more disappointments could he take? He turned his eyes once more beseechingly toward heaven.

The sun visor.

He pulled it down and a set of keys attached to a rabbit's foot by a chain fell into his lap. The keys made a tiny clink, but David heard an angelic choir.

It took a lot of grinding and screeching, but he at last got the gear shifter into a position that caused forward motion, popped the clutch and screamed away toward Lakeview Road.

41

After Blaney bashed their comrade in the face, one might have expected Josh Waley or one of the other nearby Free-to-Carry members might have chosen to shoot him. They were freely carrying firearms, after all, and that's what firearms are for. But in the actual moment, Waley and a nearby compatriot forgot all about their firearms and merely pounced on Blaney, having automatically chosen to beat the shit out of him rather than shoot the shit out of him.

Ironically, their freely-carried firearms dangling from their chests actually hindered them in their endeavor. When Blaney twisted violently, trying to break free, his hip drove the barrel of the compatriot's rifle, dangling there in front of him, into the man's crotch, smacking his testicles with such force that he was effectively removed from the fight before it had really gotten started. This left Waley alone hanging onto Blaney's back like a schoolchild very inept at leapfrog. Blaney twisted this way and that, trying to throw him off.

Jeremy had certainly not anticipated getting such action-packed video at the Rally to Keep Tennessee Safe for Christianity. This was pure virality. *Suck it, 8K camera guy!* He was so intent on his viewfinder that he was oblivious to the rising scream of the approaching pickup truck or the rising terror of the people around him who were watching said pickup truck bear down on them.

Blaney had gotten the measure of the man on his back now, and realized that neither twisting nor throwing elbows was going to dislodge him. Blaney's cap was askew and his sunglasses had been knocked off. His face was a frightening mask of rage. Turning his head sharply, he located Waley's face just over his shoulder and viciously jabbed the barrel of his rifle toward it. It connected directly with Waley's left eye. With a shriek of pain, Waley let go and was flung aside, landing on his pal, who was rolling on the ground holding his crotch. Three of the Free-Carriers were now hors de combat.

Blaney returned his attention to the newly arrived SUV and Raymond Dumond, who had just stepped out of it. He continued toward them, raising his rifle to port arms, giving every indication that he was about to take aim. The only thing blocking his shot now was Jeremy with his camera. "Get out of my God damn way, you–"

At this point the roar and screech of the approaching truck finally reached such a level that neither he nor Jeremy were any longer able to remain oblivious to it. Blaney swung to his right with his rifle, Jeremy to his left with his camera. The people between them and the roadway scampered aside in both directions, clearing a path for the onrushing truck which had swerved away from the SUV and was now heading straight for them.

42

One would think that after the time David Burkitt had spent in Rolly Blaney's truck over the last 24 hours he would by now have known the difference between the brake and the clutch. This turned out not to be the case. As he approached the black SUV at speed, he frantically stomped with both feet on what he thought was the brake. When this did not cause the truck to slow down, he tried to address the problem by stomping again, harder this time. To his dismay, this, if anything, made the problem worse. When he finally abandoned that pedal as hopeless and switched to the other, it was too late. He was definitely going to hit the SUV. To avoid this, he jerked the steering wheel to the left, which took him toward the crowd. Horrified faces flashed before him as people dove out of his path. Having now found the brake pedal, he stood up on it, and the tires locked and screamed, the scream changing to a rasping roar as the truck left the pavement. He had a split-second image of a man holding a gun, and in another split-even-smaller second he recognized Jeremy, camera raised, slightly to one side.

In its adrenaline-fueled, panic-electrified state, David's mind spat out, *My God. He's wearing another different t-shirt.*

Then there was the trailer before him, people leaping off in all directions. All the people, that is, except the State Legislator. He was poised unmoving next to the mic stand like a captain at the wheel going down with his flatbed. He would later characterize this as his icy calm and stoic courage. He was, in fact, simply petrified.

David closed his eyes and braced for impact.

43

Jeremy couldn't believe his luck. He got absolutely spectacular video of the truck skidding through the crowd and into the trailer. He even caught the ambulatory Free-to-Carry Tennessee members yanking their stricken comrades out of harm's way at the last second. The truck had slowed from its full highway speed, but still slammed into the rear corner of the flatbed with a thunderous crash. The crash was followed by a shriek of feedback as both of the loud-speakers on the trailer bounced into the air and fell off, one onto the ground, the other onto the hood of the pickup truck. The stoic/petrified legislator flipped into the air in a half somersault, landed on his head, and did a passable imitation of a breakdancer before coming to rest amid a tangle of folding chairs.

Jeremy wasn't sure what had become of Rolly Blaney. He last saw him standing directly in the truck's path, rifle half-raised, then he was gone. He might be on the other side of the truck, or he might be under it. Panning around the chaotic scene it appeared that, other than possibly Blaney, there seemed to be no serious casualties, unless there were sprains or breaks among the dignitaries who had swan dived off the flatbed. And, of course, there was the driver. *No way,* Jeremy thought, *that guy wasn't hurt.*

That guy was, in fact, hurt.

Upon impact, David flew forward over the steering wheel, and his head smacked the windshield, leaving a web of cracks in the glass. He was knocked momentarily senseless. The blow did not fracture his skull, but did split his scalp, which gushed blood.

Automatically, even before he became more or less conscious again, he began clawing at the handle on the truck's door. It swung open, and he fell out and onto the ground like a sack of wet laundry. He dragged himself to his feet using the side of the truck for support. Acrid smoke from the truck's incinerated engine and steam from its punctured radiator filled the air. People were wailing and running in all directions. In a literature class he took in college David had read *Dante's Inferno.* Now, coming into bleary, more-or-less consciousness, his sight smeared and blurred by the blood in his eyes, he thought he might have landed there. In what he guessed to be the Seventh Circle, or possibly the Fifth.

He saw what looked like a squad of infantry dragging wounded comrades away through the murk, and his mind shifted him from an inmate in Dante's Hell into an extra in *Apocalypse Now.* The throbbing in his head did sort of sound like helicopters. But the mental ramble through literature and cinema caused by his serious blow to the head was terminated abruptly by what he saw next.

Rolly Blaney rose up before him out of the red mist. He was mud-spattered, and his left arm hung at his side at an unnatural angle. In his right hand, its butt tucked into his right armpit, he held a rifle. His eyes were red with pain and rage, and his mouth was twisted in a grimace of hate. He said something short, sharp and doubtless obscene, but David couldn't make it out over all the yelling and the thumping in his head. He thought Blaney might be about to shoot him, but instead the frightening apparition swiveled and stomped toward the rear of the pickup truck.

David remembered then that he had come here because of Blaney. He had come here specifically to *stop* Blaney. He lurched after the receding form, but the moment he stepped away from the truck he fell flat on the ground, his legs having completely failed to obey.

Jeremy, on the opposite side of the truck, jerked his camera bag around from where it had slid off his shoulder and moved closer to the road and the black SUV, the better to get a wider shot of the action around the truck. Raymond Dumond still stood near the SUV's open rear door, nonplussed by the mayhem. Jeremy felt he should acknowledge the minister's presence and comment upon the astonishing turn of events. "Hey, Reverend Dumond!" he said. "Isn't this a–" He stopped. Someone else was there, he saw, inside on the back seat of the SUV. "Hey!" he said, "There's–"

"What the fuck?" shouted Reverend Dumond. He was looking past Jeremy toward the pickup truck. Jeremy turned. Emerging from the smoke was Rolly Blaney, staggering toward them, rifle raised.

"Dumond!" Blaney yelled. "There you are! And I see you in there, you bitch!" He stopped, braced himself and awkwardly took aim.

Reverend Dumond shouted, "Jesus!" He grabbed Jeremy by the shoulders and jerked him sideways, pulling Jeremy's body in front of his own. Jeremy managed to say one more, "Hey!" as the rifle went off. He jerked from the bullet's impact and fell to the ground.

Blaney, still advancing and cursing loudly, worked frantically at operating the bolt on his rifle with his one good hand. Dumond hopped over Jeremy's limp form, turned, and took off, one beautiful (definitely Italian) loafer shooting into the air like Cinderella's slipper as he sprinted away down the road.

Blaney gave up on the rifle and tossed it away. He drew the pistol from the holster on his belt and advanced. He stopped six feet away from the open back door of the SUV and raised the weapon.

44

When the truck came screaming past the police car and careened toward the people across the road, Brother Birdsong released his grip on the dancing, pink-haired girl, and centrifugal force sent her careening backward into the crowd next to the road. The girl and several others tumbled to the ground, a small shower of cellphones springing into the air and raining down around them.

Brother Birdsong watched in amazement as the truck attempted and failed to stop, swerved and drove into the crowd. The final collision was hidden from his view by the SUV, but he heard the crash and saw the hapless State Legislator do his funky dance. He could not tell the scale of the disaster from his vantage point. From where he stood it looked as though dozens might have been run down.

The policemen scattered along the yellow stripe in the middle of the road seemed as shocked and paralyzed as anyone else, though all of them did slap hands onto the butts of their service pistols, a reflexive act their training told them was suitable to almost any situation. When they did start to move toward the trouble, they found their progress impeded by people fleeing the trouble. The crowd boiled out into the road, blocking their approach.

Brother Birdsong started toward the scene of the crash. The only other disaster he had direct experience with was when a tornado tore through the area a couple of years earlier, but then he had gone out to offer solace after the fact; he hadn't been a first responder. He tried to call up memories of a first aid class he had taken once. Those memories having long since faded, he switched his mental efforts to prayer.

Halfway across the road he, like the deputies, was enveloped by the fleeing, panicked crowd. From behind him the crowd on his side also surged into the road, intent on getting a better look at what happened. Lakeview Road was a boiling cauldron of people fleeing in one direction and barging in in another.

A rifle shot rang out.

The crowd ducked as though a single entity, and the road took on the character of an anthill struck by a bootheel. Brother Birdsong, one of the few including at least some of the police officers, guns now drawn, who continued trying to reach the accident scene, was knocked this way and that. A roar went up around him. When he emerged into the open near the black SUV, stumbling and almost falling, three sheriff's deputies were standing nearby.

A figure staggered into view around the rear of the vehicle. A man covered in blood and holding a pistol. As the policemen shouted orders and a new cry of dismay arose from those people still looking on from the roadway, the man with the gun turned toward them.

45

David lost consciousness again for a moment when he hit the ground after reaching for Blaney, but yanked himself back into wakefulness by sheer effort of will. He had to stay awake. Where had Blaney gone? He had to get up. He had to move.

Once more using the side of the truck for support, he got to his feet and staggered toward the rear bumper. There were people nearby now, people very upset at having been nearly run down. They shouted at him. A red-faced woman shook a fist in his face. To David they registered as harpies. *Definitely Seventh Circle,* he thought.

As he rounded the rear of the truck, a gunshot split the air. The harpies ducked their heads and scattered like demonic quail.

The sound of the shot had an electrifying effect on David. His vision cleared. He forgot the pain. He looked in the direction of the sound and saw Rolly Blaney shuffling toward a large, black vehicle—the one he had nearly rammed a few moments earlier. Someone was lying on the ground next to the SUV. His heart skipped. Who was that? Was he too late? He let go of the truck's tailgate, shifted his weight forward on his wobbly legs and began to run, or rather stagger in a fair imitation of a run, toward the SUV.

Blaney stopped outside the vehicle's back door and aimed the pistol into it. He could have fired. He had time. But he felt the need to make one last witty comment, a la Clint Eastwood, or more realistically considering Blaney's idea of wit, Steven Seagal.

"This is what you get," he said through clenched teeth, "when you—"

David, more projectile than person at this point, thudded into his back at full tilt. Blaney lurched forward, his forehead slamming into the top of the SUV's door frame. David fell against the side of the vehicle, and seeing the weapon in Blaney's hand, grabbed at it and wrenched it away. He encountered no resistance, as Blaney was unconscious and in the process of collapsing onto the ground next to Jeremy.

David pushed himself away from the vehicle. He looked into the back seat and caught a glimpse, just a tiny, momentary glimpse, of a face looking back at him. In a half-swoon he lost his balance and staggered backwards, still holding the pistol. He managed to stop just past the rear of the SUV. His head swam. His ears rang. He made a half-turn and waved his arms, trying to regain his equilibrium.

"Glenda?" he said.

Then the deputies shot him.

46

Heaven was nice.

It was much as David thought it would be: White and shiny, warm and comfortable. There was no feeling of passing time, no physical sensation at all, really. Best of all, there were no distinct memories of his time on Earth. There was only a vague shadow of a past he could not recall, and a soft sense of relief in the knowledge that, whatever it had been, it no longer mattered. It was all behind him now, and he need not worry about it anymore.

Peaceful. That was the word. Peaceful.

Peace was all he wanted. It was all he had ever really wanted, wasn't it? That much about his previous existence he was fairly sure of. Peace! That, and naps. He wanted lots of naps, too, and Heaven, happily, turned out to be largely composed of naps. It was, indeed, Paradise.

His only complaint, as odd as it sounded to have a complaint about Heaven at all, was how Jesus kept calling him "Dave."

47

David had it wrong.

Though he had passed through a few in the air ambulance that transported him there, he lay not on a cloud, but on a bed in a hospital in Memphis. The ethereal white glow he perceived during his brief snatches of seeing anything at all was generated by Sylvania Cool White fluorescent tubes, and the enveloping sense of comforting warmth he felt was caused by a heavy blanket. His blissful feeling of contentment and forgetfulness was not the result of God's eternal love, but of large doses of strong narcotics.

In short, David was not dead. Of all the heavenly sensations he imagined he was aware of, only the naps were real.

He might have ended up in Heaven (if there is one) rather than a hospital but for the fact that several of the counter-protesters present at the Rally to Keep Tennessee Safe for Christianity were Emergency Medical Technician trainees at the nearby college, thrilled at the opportunity to use David for extra credit. It was also lucky that none of the state police present had been in a position to shoot at him; they were better trained than the county officers. Not to disparage the county officers—they would almost certainly have managed to send David to actual Heaven (if there is one) had Brother Horace Birdsong not bravely run into the line of fire to intervene.

Memphis being nowhere near Heaven, and the Second Coming having not yet occurred, the entity which insisted on calling David "Dave" was not Jesus Christ, Son of God, Savior; it was just Jeremy, Chief Engineer, T-shirt Aficionado. During the first part of David's lengthy hospital stay, Jeremy visited often to harangue the semi-conscious, heavily medicated invalid with details about things that had transpired during and since all the hooraw at the Rally to Keep Tennessee Safe for Christianity. Things, that is, which had happened to Jeremy.

Jeremy had also been shot that day by Rolly Blaney, but unlike David he was shot only once, and very unlike David he suffered only two cracked ribs. The bullet which might otherwise have killed him had been stopped just short of doing so by the extra batteries in the camera bag slung across his chest. Jeremy considered this a Miracle. In addition to extending Its hand to save his life, Providence had smiled on Jeremy in other ways, all of which he cheerfully enumerated before David's prone form. At the point at which he was knocked out by the blow from the bullet, he had already captured video of practically the entire hooraw, including a truly cinematic P.O.V. angle on his own shooting. Then, after he himself was down and out, Jeremy's camera continued to roll, having landed (miraculously?) such that it had a canted angle on David's intervention in Blaney's rampage and even, down in one corner, some of David's own bullet-riddling after he stumbled past the black SUV's rear bumper into the line of sight of the primed-to-shoot-something police officers.

Jeremy's video was unique. There were a plethora of shaky cellphone videos, but nobody got anything like Jeremy's angle on events. Even the broadcast people, caught on the other side of the road when the action started, had to settle for getting some "Tell me what you saw" interviews, including a hostile "No comment!" from a battered, swollen, and now uncharacteristically reticent Josh Whaley when asked how a squad of Good Guys With Guns had failed to intervene as promised upon the appearance of a Bad Guy with one.

Jeremy's footage was video gold, and he had subsequently sold it to multiple news outlets, converting it into a fairly impressive amount of actual gold. The money was nice, but Jeremy's greatest satisfaction was in knowing that the hotshot from the Great Rock Church with the 8K camera got diddly-squat.

"Wait 'til you see it, Dave!" Jeremy said to David's inert form, and, unable to wait himself though he had already seen it literally hundreds of times, he held his phone up and played the video in front of David's unseeing eyes.

David's sister, Donna, who flew in from Dallas as soon as she got the news, finally had Jeremy banned from the hospital.

As events transpired and consequences followed events, as his mother and father hurried in from Arizona and his sister howled for revenge, as criminal charges were considered, filed against some and dropped against others, as a media frenzy rose and fell, David lay oblivious. With the multiple surgeries required to plug all the various holes and repair the numerous rips and tears, he remained Rip Van Winkle through it all.

When he finally regained enough awareness of his surroundings to understand that, as previously mentioned, he wasn't actually dead, the realization was one of the greatest disappointments of his life.

<h1 style="text-align:center">48</h1>

Jeremy, it turned out, and not for the first time by any means, was not entirely accurate in all of his assumptions. The hotshot 8K camera guy from the Great Rock Church Media Department had in fact acquired somewhat more than diddly-squat. It was true that he had leaned on the fender of his car videoing diddly-squat for quite a while that morning, but that was because his remit was strictly to capture footage of Reverend Raymond Dumond, the rest of the proceedings being of little interest to his boss, Reverend Raymond Dumond. When the black SUV appeared, he stood up and went into action, moving into the area in front of the stage to record Reverend Dumond's triumphant arrival and ascent to the microphone. Once the pickup truck came barreling in and the hooraw began in earnest, his footage became pretty wild and shaky, understandably, given all the pandemonium. He did manage to steady his shot, however, for a few crucial seconds immediately prior to and immediately following the first gunshot.

Reviewing this footage later, 8K Guy realized that he had something that might very well be of some interest to the general public. He also realized that it was something that Raymond Dumond might be very loath to have seen by the general public. Following all the excitement, Reverend Dumond made many statements to many media outlets about his actions during all the hooraw—actions involving quick thinking, lightning reflexes, steely bravery in the face of physical danger and so on. None of these actions, it turned out, were evident in 8K Guy's gorgeous, super-high resolution, 60-frames-per-second video. Being a reasonable and basically nice guy, 8K Guy felt it only fair to give Reverend Dumond the opportunity to make the call about what should be done with the video. All 8K Guy asked, not unreasonably, was a small consideration for his diligence and loyalty.

Say, oh, I don't know... Fifty thousand dollars?

There commenced a period of haggling which was not without some bitterness on the part of Reverend Dumond. When the haggling was done, 8K Guy got his fifty thousand dollars, which was delivered in cash in a somewhat comically cloak-and-dagger manner involving coded messages, unconvincing disguises, and rendezvous in public places. The money delivered, the camera's memory card was duly handed over to the red-faced reverend as promised.

Then, because Dumond was such an asshole, 8K Guy posted the video, a copy of which he had naturally kept, on YouTube anyway.

The footage quite clearly showed Reverend Raymond Dumond grabbing a young man to use as a human shield and then, as the deranged gunman approached his SUV, fleeing the scene in a manner which would be described variously in YouTube comments as resembling that of a scared rabbit, a scalded dog, and "Usain Bolt with his ass on fire."

The public airing of the video caused some small embarrassment for the Reverend. This embarrassment was prolonged when the footage subsequently went viral over and over again as various people re-edited multiple versions of it with different soundtracks. These included music such as the Benny Hill Theme, as well as bits of sound from various cartoons, including the "meep-meep/richochet" sound effect from the Roadrunner and flapping feet followed by the screamed "Wait for meeee!!" from Scooby-doo. The final version, a clever re-framing of the gag, was Reverend Dumond's headlong flight put into slow motion accompanied by the theme from the 1981 film, *Chariots of Fire.*

Reverend Dumond's headlong flight was subsequently also separated entirely from its context and turned into an animated meme, one which promised to be useful forevermore to illustrate such common situations as, "My husband when it's time to change a diaper," or "Me when my friend asks me to help him move."

Reverend Dumond's uncomfortable public scrutiny continued and even increased when some people, their deference perhaps lessened after watching the Reverend flee danger to the sound of Chuck Berry's *Run Run Rudolph*, began to question what exactly was being done with all the money raised through donations to the Campaign to Keep Tennessee Safe for Christianity. Reverend Dumond was able to counter suggestions that the money pledged to Keep Tennessee Safe for Christianity had possibly been misused by pointing to a raft of evidence indicating that Christianity in Tennessee was, in fact, still pretty safe.

Under fire in this way, Reverend Dumond loudly declared all of these attacks to be bolts fired at him by Satan himself, the Evil One being intent on interfering with the Reverend's Godly works. In completely eschewing any personal responsibility and laying it all off on infernal influences, he was unknowingly echoing Deion's Succubus Theory of Infidelity, though without the mitigating circumstance of Deion's unfortunate blood sugar levels.

In the midst of all this, Reverend Dumond announced that he would be taking a sabbatical from The Great Rock Church to refresh his faith and to seek inspiration among the sacred sites of the Holy Land, where he would be traveling for some time.

Pre-Epilogue

David stood alone in his kitchen. In his hand was a small, heavy object which he contemplated, brow furrowed, like Hamlet studying Yorick's skull. The object was a small, impressively detailed model of a Coca-Cola vending machine. He turned it in his hand, admiring the workmanship. After a few more moments of silent consideration, he dropped it into the open cardboard shipping box on the table in front of him, closed the flaps and reached for the packing tape. This was the last bit of memorabilia in the last box.

If only, he thought, *I could get rid of actual memories this easily.*

He had spent weeks in the hospital undergoing multiple surgeries and then recovering from them, and had now been home nearly two weeks. It had taken those two weeks to convince his sister Donna and his parents that he would be fine on his own. Heaven knew he appreciated their help and concern. Donna especially had looked out for him and his interests while he was dead to the world, dealing with doctors and lawyers and everything else while shuttling back and forth between Memphis and Dallas, where she had a job and a family of her own. Heaven knew he couldn't have made it without them. Heaven also knew how glad he was to see them go.

Everyone was very solicitous when he finally came around. *Don't bother him! Don't tire him out!* But he could see the questions in their eyes and could feel the strain of the Herculean effort necessary to hold them back. Eventually, he knew, the dam would have to break, and the commiseration would turn to interrogation. When it finally did, it appeared the flood would never ebb.

His mother broke first. "What happened, David? *Something* must have happened." Her hand gripped his, her voice was filled with concern and a certain tinge of *come on, you can tell* me. Variations on this theme continued to pop up intermittently the entire time she remained in Tennessee. *Something* must have happened! Glenda was such a nice girl! Such a perfect sweetheart. There must be some explanation, some catalyst, some trigger, and, most importantly, someone to blame.

"What," his father asked when he was left alone with David in the hospital room, "the hell did you *do*?" He didn't seem to find David's protests of innocence convincing. One possible reason became clear when his father leaned closer and lowered his voice to a harsh whisper. "I heard you were drunk. In the *church*! Is that true?"

His father had heard it? How had his father heard it? If his father *had heard it, then everyone...* The conversation was cut short at that point by an alarm going off on David's heart monitor.

David picked up the cardboard box and took it into the laundry room with the others stacked three deep and covering most of the floor. He had no idea what he was going to do with it all. His father had declared that the junk must be worth something and he should sell it. His sister had suggested various options including dumping it all loose in the parking lot of the Great Rock Church. David decided to simply not decide.

He came back into the kitchen and wondered if he should have lunch. It was almost lunchtime, so that seemed like a proper course of action. He had lost a lot of weight in the hospital, and one of the promises his mother had extracted as a condition of leaving him on his own was that he would not skip meals. You shouldn't break a promise you made to your mother. Sacred vows and all that. Maybe he would have a glass of tea and some crackers.

He glanced down at the space at the end of the counter where Bitsy's food bowl used to sit. Bitsy was certainly not one to ever miss a meal. He hoped she was getting plenty to eat now. If not, he was sure there would be hell to pay, wherever she was. Shortly after Donna arrived, she went to check on his house. Once David was coherent, she reported that she had found the kitchen "trashed out." That, he knew about already. She also found a note on the kitchen counter. "What the heck does this mean?" she asked.

Dear David, it read. *Fuck you. I'm taking her cat. Laura.*

"It's complicated," he replied.

Looking at the empty space, he smiled to himself. He certainly never thought he would miss the hostile little creature. And he didn't.

The telephone rang.

It rang from time to time. No danger now, at least, of any capitalized calls. Though the media excitement over the hooraw during the Rally to Keep Tennessee Safe for Christianity had died down, public curiosity having moved on to other scandals and outrages, he still got calls from time to time from journalists, people who imagined they were journalists, simple nosy-parkers and lawyers looking to get in on a lawsuit against the county or anybody else they could think of. David answered no call at all unless the caller I.D. indicated it was his sister or his parents, and he wouldn't have answered those except that failure to do so would cause more trouble than answering did.

When he looked at the I.D. for this call, he did a double-take. The caller indicated was so surprising that his curiosity overcame his reticence, and he picked up the phone. A recorded voice announced that he was receiving a collect call and that, should he accept the call, it would be logged and recorded.

David dithered a moment. Curiosity won out again, and he pressed "1" to accept.

Epilogue

David stared at the poster on the wall. The prohibited actions and activities listed on it were numerous and varied, and he had finished reading them some time ago. Now it was merely a place to look while he waited. It had taken a while to get through the various checks and the metal detector with the line of other visitors, and he was glad to at least be able to sit down. The room was large and reminiscent of a high school cafeteria—tile floor, blank cinder block walls, a grid of tables with plastic-backed chairs spaced at not-quite-private distances. Instead of teachers, however, the room was watched over by hard-eyed, uniformed guards.

There had been a low-level roar of voices when the doors first opened and the inmates came in, which had now receded to a murmur. "His" inmate had not been in that group. Three other sets of visitors sat nearby. One was a lone man in a suit, presumably someone's lawyer, whose inmate had also not come out yet, and who kept looking at his watch. The other two were families; wives or significant others with their children. One of the women arrived with two girls who both looked to be under twelve. The other woman brought along a sullen teenaged boy who wore a hoodie with the hood up and who sat, shoulders hunched, hands in pockets until their prisoner was brought out and he reluctantly submitted to a hug.

David sighed.

The beautiful day for a drive had belied the grimness of his destination. The last few miles were especially nice, flanked as they were by cottonfields just coming into bloom. People didn't usually think of cottonfields as pretty, except perhaps when they were busting out all white, but David found these with their scattered, tiny spots of color to be lovely. When the high fences and ominous buildings came into view across the fields and the turn to the gate came into view, he was tempted to just keep driving. The Mississippi River was not much farther away down this same road. He could find a spot on the bluff, sit in the sunshine and look at the water. He had a feeling that might turn out to have been a better use of his time.

But he had turned in at the gate, and now here he was. A guard opened the door in the far wall and stepped aside. Four more men walked into the room. One of them was Rolly Blaney.

For a moment David did not recognize him. The formerly close-cropped hair had grown out. He now sported a dark, bushy beard with two streaks of gray running down from the corners of his mouth. He reminded David of Charlton Heston halfway through *The Ten Commandments.* He wore the same denim trousers and blue shirt with TDOC stenciled on it as the other men in the room. As he neared David's table, he grinned a sardonic grin. That much, at least, was familiar. "Jesus, Burkitt," he said. "You look like shit." That was familiar, too.

"You look great," David said. "Next time, you get shot and I'll go to jail."

Blaney seemed a bit surprised by the snappy comeback. With an amused grunt he pulled out the chair and sat down at the table opposite David. "Gotta tell ya, I didn't expect you to really come out here," he said.

"I said I would." David tapped a fingernail on the scarred table-top. "It's against my better judgment. But here I am."

"Wanna hear something funny? A friend of yours has already been out."

David looked up. "Really?" he said suspiciously. "Who would that be?"

"Birdsong." Blaney laughed quietly.

David blinked in surprise. "Brother Birdsong came here?"

"Yeah. How do you like that? I started to blow him off. Figured he was here to save my soul or some shit. Or maybe just to rub it in." He slouched in his chair. "But it ain't like I have a lot else on my calendar, so I talked to him. What do you think he wanted?" Blaney laughed again. "Wanted to know if I *needed* anything! Said he knew I didn't have nobody on the outside, and could he help any way. That's all. That's all he wanted." Blaney shook his head in amusement. "So I said, well, O.K., yeah. I could use some socks and underwear. This prison issue shit is wore-out and scratchy. He said, OK. I kept waiting for the catch, naturally." Blaney paused. David waited. "Son of bitch sent me a bunch of drawers and socks." He hitched a leg up and thumped a sneakered foot onto the tabletop, hiked up his pant leg to show a white crew sock. "What do you think of that?"

"Brother Birdsong," said David, "is a good Christian. They do exist."

Blaney dropped his foot to the floor once more. "If you say so."

There was a moment of silence. A voice from one of the other tables said, "Listen to your moms!" and was answered by a mumble. Blaney glanced in that direction. David finally spoke. "All right. You said you wanted to tell me something."

"Yeah. And I don't like talking on them jailhouse phones."

"Here I am. What is it?"

Blaney's expression became sly. He wasn't ready to get to the point yet. "So I guess you got to be the hero, huh?" he said. "Saving the day and catching the bad guy and all. It's just like the fucking Boyd County cops to shoot the hero!" He laughed. David remained deadpan. "Bet you're suing the shit out of 'em."

"Their liability insurance is helping with my hospital bills."

"That's it?" Blaney said, aghast. "You're gonna just leave all that money on the table?" Blaney seemed unable to grasp such a concept.

Then his eyes narrowed again. "You know, come to think of it, maybe I ought to sue *you*. For wrecking my truck. Busting my arm." He worked his arm, which had obviously healed completely. "Not to mention that concussion you give me."

"Sure," said David. "And Jeremy can sue *you*. For shooting him."

Blaney shrugged elaborately. "He lived. Anyway, not my fault!"

"Right. Not your fault. All you did was pull the trigger."

"Not my fault I shot *him*. He got in the way."

"What do you want, Blaney?" David's voice had risen and some of the others, including the man in the suit, looked their way.

Blaney's chuckles faded away. He leaned forward and rested his elbows on the table. "All right. Don't get your panties in a wad. It ain't that big a deal, really. I just wanted to thank you."

David frowned. Had he missed something? "Thank me? For what?"

"For being Mr. Hero."

David stared at him. "I don't understand you."

Blaney looked down at the table, rapped it absently with a knuckle. "Well, it's like this. Fact of business, you done me a favor. If I had managed to do what I went there to do, they'd 'a had me for capital murder. No question. That is, if the cops didn't do to me what they tried to do to you. So I guess I'd be dead right now, or on death row. As it is," he shrugged. "A plea deal on a couple of counts of attempted and some piddly assault shit? I'll get out of here while my pecker still works." He looked up at David. "They give me a Jew lawyer, too. That helped."

David felt his strength begin to ebb. This was taking more out of him than he had anticipated. "And all this is only occurring to you now?" he said. "Why in God's name did you try to do it in the first place?"

"I was pretty pissed off," he said simply. "And, truth be told, I maybe wasn't making the wisest decisions. You don't tend to when you're on meth."

David sat up. "You were on meth?"

"Oh yeah," Blaney said, nodding. "'Specially right there at the end. Had me a little fucked up. That," his expression became sly once more, "along with everything else." David thought he knew what was coming, but Blaney threw him another curveball. "What do you hear from what's-her-name? The one you were banging in the choir loft?"

David flinched. He looked around, checking to make sure no one had heard. "Laura," he said. He did not correct Blaney's error as to the precise location. "I don't hear anything."

"No? When I left her at your house, she looked like she was moving in."

"She took the cat and left. I haven't seen or heard from her, and I don't want to."

Blaney squinted at him. "She took the cat?"

"It's complicated."

"Uh huh," said Blaney. *Here it comes*, David thought. "And what about..." Blaney laughed. "I almost said, Trixie."

David's face clouded, but after a moment he relaxed. Anger simply required too much energy. He sighed. "Nothing. Well, that isn't quite true. Divorce papers were in the pile of mail when I got home."

Blaney's jaw dropped. "You gotta be shitting me." His voice was so loud this time that everyone nearby turned to look. "You come swinging in like Tarzan, save her life, get shot up doing it, and all you get is a, 'Sign here?' Anyway, if anybody was filing papers, it shoulda been you." David said nothing. "Holy shit. What about Dumond?"

"What about him?"

Blaney's voice took on a tinge of desperation. "O.K., maybe she didn't come back to you, but... I mean, she seen him run off and leave her. Don't tell me..." His expression was pleading. David merely smiled sadly. "Forget what I said," Blaney said at last. "God damn that punk Jeremy. Why did he have to get in the way?"

David drew a few circles on the tabletop with an index finger. "I would think you would admire Dumond. Playing all the suckers like he did. By all accounts that little crusade against the Muslims you handed him made him a lot of money. I guess that makes you a sucker, too."

The door opened and another inmate was led in, this one going to the table where the presumed lawyer was waiting. "About damn time," said the man in the suit, and the two put their heads together. David sat impassively, a slight smile on his lips. Blaney, glowering, said, "You seem to be taking it all pretty good."

David considered a reply. Looking across the table at the man facing him, he pondered the absurdity of this situation. Of all the people to find himself about to confide in, crude, bigoted, atheistic, quite possibly psychopathic Rolly Blaney was one he would have placed very near the bottom of the list. He hadn't even been able to confide in Brother Birdsong when the minister dutifully visited him in the hospital. Upon hearing the preacher's voice speaking to his sister outside the room, for a few panicked moments David had even considered feigning unconsciousness. Following Brother Birdsong's greeting and a rather long and uncomfortable silence, David had finally only managed to squeeze out a whispered, "I'm sorry." Brother Birdsong shook his head and said, "No, David, I'm the one who's sorry. I handled the whole thing badly. I should have done something as soon as I...knew."

"You tried," David murmured. "The woman at the well?"

"Ah," said Brother Birdsong. "Yes. A bit too subtle, in hindsight. But I considered the story of the woman taken in adultery..."

"A little," said David, "too 'on the nose?'"

Another uncomfortable silence, a pat on the arm, and Brother Birdsong left.

David had not had the courage to ask after the health of Mrs. Birdsong.

So he hadn't even been able to talk to Brother Birdsong. Yet... A moment ago, for the first time since their ill-fated acquaintance began, David thought he saw a different kind of look in Blaney's eyes. A look that was neither of rage nor disdain. So he spoke.

"After I ran into you and knocked you down," David said, and frowned down at the meaningless figures his index finger was tracing on the table, "I saw her in there. In the back seat of that car. Just for a second, but I saw her. And she saw me. I looked at her eyes, and... I didn't know her. I mean, it was Glenda, but it wasn't *my* Glenda. It came into my mind in that second that... Maybe my Glenda never even existed. I don't know. But right then, at that second, I somehow realized that I had to let it all go. Just...let it go." He took a breath and continued more quickly. "In the hospital when I turned out not to be dead, I was sorry at first. Sorry I wasn't dead, I mean. But there were people there who were glad I wasn't dead. So. I decided I'd go on living. And just let things be the way they are." He suddenly felt embarrassed by his own earnestness. He gave a little laugh. "And that's that. Now I think I'd better go. I may drive down and look at the River for a while, since I'm so close."

Blaney stared at him intensely for a long moment, then began to slowly nod his head. "You know what, Burkitt?" he said solemnly. David looked up and met Blaney's earnest gaze. "You and me? We're just a couple of hopeless romantics."

They sat in silence for a long moment, then a voice nearby said, "That's what I'm paying you for!" It was the convict with the impatient lawyer. David scooted his chair back from the table and stood. "OK then. I'm going to go now." He paused. "Is there... Is there anything I can do for you?" He tried to make his tone light. "Need any more socks or underwear?"

As though waking from a trance, Blaney sat back in his chair and the cloudy mood in his eyes was replaced by the familiar sharp look of disdain. "You're a 'good Christian,' too, huh, Burkitt?" he smirked.

The question took David aback for a moment. "To tell you the truth," he said, "I really don't know anymore."

Blaney squinted at him. "Yeah," he drawled. "I reckon you are." His hairy face broke into a wide grin. "Long as you can leave the bottle alone and stay out of the choir loft."

"Goodbye, Rolly," David said.

Blaney's laughter echoed after him as he left the day room.

The water in the Mississippi was brown, but the sunlight on it made it sparkle nonetheless. David looked at it for a long time before getting back in his car and driving home.

Post-Epilogue

As a rule, Reverend Raymond Dumond did not care for Mexicans. For one thing, most of them are Catholic. And for another, all of them are Mexican. But Cozumel wasn't really *Mexico* Mexico, and after all, when visiting Mexico, allowances must be made perforce. At any rate, he didn't mind the Mexican in the white coat approaching with his piña colada.

"Thank you, Pedro," he said as the waiter, whose name was Benicio, set the drink on the table next to his lounge chair. "And when the lady gets here, do be sure to bring her rum and Coke."

"Of course, *Señor* Duchamps," said Benicio. Reverend Dumond and his companion were traveling at the moment as Mr. & Mrs. Peter Duchamps. Things were just...simpler that way.

Reverend/Not-a-Reverend Dumond/Duchamps picked up his drink and sucked at the straw. Before him the gleaming white sand was so shining, the blue of the Caribbean so vivid, that the view might have hurt his eyes but for the three-hundred-dollar sunglasses he wore. He glanced at his shockingly expensive watch and frowned. Shouldn't she have been here by now?

The undercover Reverend had felt the need for total relaxation after all the stress thrown his way during the last few weeks before leaving Tennessee. The thought of it caused a momentary twinge and tightening in his gut even now, and he took a deep, cleansing breath and another sip of piña colada to head off the memory. He consoled himself with the knowledge that others in his line had bounced back from worse. Time heals all wounds, and by the time he returned from "the Holy Land" all of it would have blown over.

His new marriage, which should hopefully be legal by that point, would be a *fait acompli* (or as his average parishioner might put it, "a done deal"), and that would be that. In the meantime, he was embracing this place's many opportunities to relax and do nothing. His traveling companion, on the other hand, had thrown herself into all the activities the resort had to offer. He frowned at the thought. It seemed as if he had barely seen her since they got there.

A shadow fell across his face. He looked up to find, to his surprise, the tawny, muscular form of Ricardo or Raoul or whatever his name was, the diving instructor. The man gave an ingratiating smile. "Excuse me, *señor*?" he said.

"Yes, what?"

"Sorry to disturb you," said Pancho or Pablo or whatever his name was. "I was just wondering..." He paused and looked around. His luxuriant mane of coal-black hair shook and fell across his brow. He pushed it away absently. "Have you seen Glenda?"

"I beg your pardon?" The man's Speedo was at eye level, which Dumond found disconcerting.

"*Señora* Duchamps? She was supposed to meet me." He looked around again, then quickly added, "For her scuba lesson!" His handsome face crinkled with worry, or possibly frustration. "But she hasn't... She didn't..." He trailed off awkwardly. Experiencing a problem with his English, no doubt.

Before *Señor* Duchamps/Dumond could formulate a reply, Benicio appeared at the scuba instructor's side carrying a tray. "*Perdoname*," he said, and with a slight, graceful bend at the waist he held the tray out before him. This time the tray held not a drink, but a small piece of paper. There was a twinkle in the waiter's eye which the Reverend found almost as disconcerting as Pancho's Speedo.

"The lady has sent you a note, *señor*."

Dumond picked it up, unfolded it and squinted at the white paper. The sun was so bright that it was hard to look at it. The letters were small and carefully inscribed.

Dear Raymond: I'm sorry to hurt you this way...

The End

Cover Design by Henderson Fish

Background Texture
Courtesy of Annie Spratt
via Unsplash.com